THE KINGS OF SUMMER

by James M. Waner

Copyright © 2015 James Waner
All rights reserved
First Edition

PAGE PUBLISHING, INC.
New York, NY

First originally published by Page Publishing, Inc. 2015

ISBN 978-1-68139-339-1 (pbk)
ISBN 978-1-68139-340-7 (digital)

Printed in the United States of America

DEDICATION

This book is dedicated to my wife, Carol,
without whose love and support it might
never have been completed.

CONTENTS

Chapter 1	Arrival in Chicago	7
Chapter 2	The Truth or Nearly So	14
Chapter 3	The First of Many Schemes	19
Chapter 4	My First Major League Game	23
Chapter 5	Big Patty's, Fawn, and Melissa	27
Chapter 6	Frieda Cooks Breakfast	32
Chapter 7	Washing the Car	36
Chapter 8	The Blind Date	39
Chapter 9	What? No Banana Split?	44
Chapter 10	The Morning after: Sunday Mass	47
Chapter 11	Misadventure at the Beach	52
Chapter 12	Frieda and Glenn Pay the Price	57
Chapter 13	Stop and Smell the Roses	60
Chapter 14	Mad Dog	63
Chapter 15	The Basketball Game	66
Chapter 16	The Folk Group Rehearsal	69
Chapter 17	Three-legged Walking	76
Chapter 18	Second Phone Call to Erica	79
Chapter 19	The Fight	82
Chapter 20	The Queen of Chinese Checkers	85

Chapter 21	The Speed Chess Tournament	90
Chapter 22	RG3 and the Death Match	93
Chapter 23	"Brains"	96
Chapter 24	The Bowling Date	99
Chapter 25	Paulo's	103
Chapter 26	The Dilemma	110
Chapter 27	Chores and Distractions	112
Chapter 28	The Softball Game	114
Chapter 29	Thank You, Mad Dog	121
Chapter 30	Uncle Fred's Surprise	125
Chapter 31	First Lessons at Riverview	128
Chapter 32	The Learning Curve	136
Chapter 33	Shopping with Kay	141
Chapter 34	The Pool Party	150
Chapter 35	The Bomb	157
Chapter 36	The Kings of Summer	163

CHAPTER 1

Arrival in Chicago

It was the summer of 1960 between my junior and senior year in high school, and I was going to visit my cousin Leon in Chicago. This was a big deal to me because it marked the first time my parents had let me travel outside the city limits of Benton Harbor by myself. I can still remember the sense of pride and independence I carried along with my luggage aboard the old South Shore Lines bus, which was to take me to Michigan City, Indiana. There I would transfer to an electric train for the remainder of the trip to Chicago. Once on the train, I read again the letters I had received from my cousins Leon and Cindy. Leon's note said:

> Joey,
>
> Hey, cousin, we are going to have a great time. The first night you are here we will be going to see the White Sox play the Yankees. Then, the next night I've got you a date with Erica who is a good friend of my girlfriend, Phyllis. Erica is kinda cute. I think you'll like her, but if not, we'll get you a different date for later in the week. Don't worry, you'll meet lots of girls while you're here. Between Cindy's

friends and the girls I know, you'll be busier than a dachshund with a hot dog tied to its bobbed tail. I have lots of other things planned too, including meeting my friend "Mad Dog" Norkus. Don't forget to pack your baseball glove and basketball shoes. Looking forward to your visit.

Leon

He said Erica was "kinda cute." At my school that means that one of us needs to be wearing a bag over our head, and if it's me wearing the bag, there will be no eye holes. I hope the Chicago code is different. On the other hand, seeing a White Sox game and meeting a guy named "Mad Dog" should prove interesting. Next I looked at the note from Cindy.

Hi Joey,

I'll also try to make sure you have a good time. I know you'll like the White Sox game and meeting "Mad Dog" will be a real treat. I think you'll like Erica. She's real nice. But if you don't, I have several friends that are anxious to meet you. I've also got a couple of things planned for your stay but I'll keep them a surprise for now. After all, you are the closest thing I have to a real cousin.

See ya soon.
Cindy

That's right, Cindy is Leon's step-sister and she has no cousins other than me and my sisters. But there it was again. "I think you'll like Erica. She's real nice." When a girl tells you that her friend is "real nice" that usually translates into having a good personality but not much for looks. Poor Erica, "kinda cute" and "real nice." This could be real awkward.

*   *   *

I felt so cool! I knew I was going to have a great time with my new-found freedom and could hardly wait as I stepped down from the train, battered suitcase in hand, walked with calm authority through the revolving doors of the station into the bright sunlight, and stride purposefully to…Oh, frogs!

I decided that since I didn't remember where I was supposed to go, I would just fake it. I'd just walk right out the front door of the station and catch the first city bus going north. I mean, how big could Chicago be? I figured by going north I was bound to see something I recognized. After all, I had been to Uncle Fred's once before—when I was six. Fortunately, I never had a chance to put this grand theory into action.

My parents, having faith enough to let me go to Chicago alone, also had a total lack of trust in my memory. They had called ahead and asked Uncle Fred and Aunt Leona to meet me at the station "just in case."

My mom always said "just in case." When I was in grade school she would say things like, "You'd better take your galoshes, just in case, dear." or "You'd better wear your sweater today, just in case, dear." To me, the phrase "just in case" meant the galoshes or the sweater would ward off some impending doom that would otherwise threaten my life. I didn't get it. Most of my classmates didn't wear galoshes or sweaters when I had to and they seemed perfectly fine to me. I guess some people are just born to worry. Finally, when I entered high school, knowing that my personal knowledge greatly surpassed that of my parents and teachers (and most other 'old folks' for that matter), I began to challenge all "just in case" statements. As I listened half-heartedly to the statement, I would attempt to make up a witty response. At that time I was already halfway to becoming a true wit. It might go something like this:

> MOM: Why don't you run over to the store and get another half-gallon of milk, just in case.
> ME: (cleverly) Oh, come on, Mom, just in case what?
> MOM: (parentally) You know what I mean. Uncle Norman is visiting this weekend, dear. I don't want to run out of milk.
> ME: (wittily) I also know Uncle Norman doesn't usually drink milk. How 'bout

I pick up a half gallon of beer.

But I'd go and get the milk anyway.

Uncle Norman was a bachelor, mainly because he never met an unmarried girl whose father owned a brewery. When he made one of his biannual trips to visit us, he would wear two complete changes of clothing, carry a small paper sack with his razor and toothbrush, and bring a gigantic suitcase, which was always completely filled with beer when he arrived and totally empty when he left. My father was always willing to help him lighten his suitcase. Mom refused to buy beer for him or even let him put his beer in the refrigerator. In the winter he would hang his suitcase out the bedroom window on his belt and during the summer visit, he would just drink warm beer. One winter it was so cold that the beer froze and most of the bottles broke. The next morning there was bright sunshine and a sudden warming trend and the beer started dripping out of the suitcase and down the side of the house. Boy, did Mom spit nails about that. Uncle Norman was ready to spit nails too, but for a different reason. Dad thought the whole thing was quite funny until spring when he had to repaint the whole house. Then he was ready to buy a second refrigerator or kill Uncle Norman.

I also remember that as I was preparing for the Chicago trip, Mom had said something about calling ahead to have someone meet me at the station "just in case." "What kind of ninny do you think I am?" I said. "I know how to get to their house. All you gotta do is have a little faith in me, Mom. Gee!" As it turned out, that's exactly what she did; she had "little faith" in me. She called ahead anyway. Thank God.

I had just stepped off the train when I heard Aunt Leona call. "Yoo-hoo, Joey. Over here!" I was both embarrassed and relieved. I ran over and suffered through the usual hugs and handshakes. Along with Aunt Leona was Uncle Fred and my cousins Frieda and Cindy. Leon wasn't there, much to my surprise. "Where's Leon?" I asked.

"Oh, he had a guitar lesson," (RAH! RAH! RAH!) said Aunt Leona. "He'll be back by the time we get home. My, haven't you grown since we last saw you." (RAH! RAH! RAH!)

"Yes, I guess I have, Aunt Leona," I said. (But I thought: Cripes! You haven't seen me since I was twelve. What did you expect, a seventeen-year-old dwarf?) Relatives are really observant. They notice that between twelve and seventeen you get taller. I would later notice that when you hit middle age, they will cleverly observe that you have "filled out," which is their way of saying that they think of you when they see Shamu the killer whale.

You may be wondering about the "RAH! RAH! RAH!" I injected earlier. Everyone knows someone like my aunt Leona who, by the way, is my dad's sister. She was a cheerleader from the moment of conception. She has a Doris Day look about her and every time she says something you want to go RAH! RAH! RAH! She could read obituaries on death row and be cheery. She was short, a little plump, terribly blonde, and always wore a pleated skirt and a pull-over sweater. I was afraid to look down to see if she was wearing saddle shoes and white socks. Of course she made the cheerleading squad from sixth grade until she graduated from high school. She started going steady with Uncle Fred when she was five. Uncle Fred didn't start going steady with her until he was sixteen. I don't know how she managed during those eleven years. They broke up about a year after graduation and each went on to marry someone else. Aunt Leona had Leon from that marriage and Uncle Fred had Cindy from his first marriage. Aunt Leona and Uncle Fred lived in Chicago suburbs quite distant from one another during their first marriages and had completely lost track of each other. It turned out that their respective spouses died within four months of one another, Aunt Leona's husband from a brain aneurysm and Uncle Fred's wife in a car accident. About two years later, they met up at a high school reunion, decided that breaking up wasn't such a good idea, and got married six months later. Together they had Frieda. Guess who suggested that name. (RAH! RAH! RAH!)

Uncle Fred was six-foot-seven and thin with wavy brown hair. He had been an all-state center on his high school basketball team as well as being involved in most of the other major sports in school. As he grew older, however, he gave up being a jock and settled for being just an average guy who happened to own a very successful landscaping business. Even so, with Aunt Leona around, he must still feel as though he is on the basketball court. He didn't seem to mind.

Frieda was the youngest at nine. She was skinny with long, stringy, brown hair and buck teeth. She was also a colossal pain a bit south of the shoulder blades. She had an annoying, whiney voice and had developed the ability to make a wide variety of rude and obnoxious noises. Her primary claim to fame was that she could make a continuous series of noises that made you feel as though you were at the epicenter of a zoo where the entire animal population had been struck mad simultaneously. When she did this, nobody admitted knowing her or how she had escaped the asylum.

Cindy was sixteen, almost seventeen and just five months younger than Leon. She had let it be known that as soon as she turned seventeen, she would reclaim the position of co-oldest. She was about five-foot-four, had shoulder-length blonde hair, blue-green eyes, and not surprisingly, commanded quite a bit of attention from guys passing by. A girl that looked like she did should not be any guy's cousin.

Having completed the usual family greetings we all piled into Uncle Fred's VW bus. They didn't need a VW bus, but Aunt Leona and Uncle Fred were den parents for nine kids who wore Cub Scout uniforms one day a week and vandalized schools, playgrounds, and public restrooms the other six days. They thought the bus would be ideal for taking the scouts on camping trips, to museums, and to ball games. They also thought it would be cute to call the bus *THE WOLF PACK TRANSPORT* since one of the badges the cub scouts earn is the Wolf badge. Judging by the looks of the bus, it's too bad there wasn't a Rabid Wart Hog badge. "You'll have to excuse the inside of the bus, Joey," said Uncle Fred after we were a few minutes away from the train station. "We took the cub scouts to see the White Sox play last night."

"I'll bet you bought them Juicy Fruit gum, didn't you?" I said. The bus literally reeked of Juicy Fruit gum.

"Why, yes, we did," replied Aunt Leona. "How did you know that?"

"Just a lucky guess," I said. "By the way, do you have a freezer at your house?"

"We do," said Uncle Fred, "why do you ask?"

"I must have sat on some gum on the train," I said. "I heard that if you put clothes with gum on them in the freezer for a while, the gum comes off easier."

Cindy, who was sitting next to me, looked at me and smiled. "Gee, you sure are smart, Joey," she said admiringly (and with amazing accuracy).

"Yeah? Well, if he's so smart, why did he sit on the gum?" sniped Frieda.

"Frieda!" exclaimed Cindy.

"Pipe down, Frieda!" said Uncle Fred.

"Now, Fred, be gentle," said Aunt Leona. "Frieda, Joey is our guest this week. (RAH! RAH! RAH!) Please try to be nice. Tell Joey you're sorry."

"I'm sorry," pouted Frieda. (Like hell she was.)

"That's OK," I said. "Forget about it." She could forget about it, but I sure wouldn't. I coughed, and while covering my mouth, I slyly removed half the gum I had been chewing. Since Frieda couldn't sit still, I knew I'd get a chance to drop some on her seat before we got to the house.

It seemed like we drove for an hour. I couldn't believe that a city could be so big. I mean, when we went somewhere in Benton Harbor, it never took more than twenty minutes to get anywhere. And that included the time it took to settle the arguments as to who was going to sit by the window and who got to ride shotgun. I made a mental note not to say anything to my mother about calling ahead.

CHAPTER 2

The Truth or Nearly So

Finally we pulled down a residential street and into a driveway. All the houses looked the same. I figured the builder must have told his crew to keep on building them using the same plans until they got it right. From the comments Uncle Fred had made to my dad over the years, Uncle Fred didn't get the one that was done right.

"Well, here we are," Uncle Fred announced. "I'll get your bag, Joey. You go on in with the others. Leon should be home by now."

As we started to get out of the bus, Frieda finally noticed. "Hey!" she screeched. "Someone put gum on my seat. I'll bet Joey did it."

"Why, Frieda, you should be ashamed of yourself." It was Aunt Leona. (No RAH! RAH! RAH! this time.) "Joey wouldn't do that. It was probably one of the scouts from last night."

"Mom's right, sis," said Cindy. "I was sitting next to Joey all the way home and I'm sure it wasn't him." She looked back at me, smiled, and winked. She had seen me do it.

"Now you tell Joey you're sorry," ordered Aunt Leona.

"I'M SORRY!" she spat out the words. I just smiled but my mind kept saying *GOTCHA!*

As we entered the house Aunt Leona was calling for Leon. Obviously Leon wasn't home yet. She called at least eleven times more. Finally she figured out what the rest of us already knew. Cindy covered her face in embarrassment. Aunt Leona turned to me and said, "I guess Leon isn't home yet." I was just now beginning to realize the limitations of the family brain trust. "Cindy, why don't you take Joey upstairs and show him where Leon's room is. Then you can come down and show him the family scrapbook."

"Oh, Mother! Not the one with all my baby pictures. You wouldn't," cried Cindy. "Joey, promise you won't look at the scrapbook, PLEASE!"

"I'm really not much into scrapbooks, Aunt Leona," I said. "Maybe you've got a *Sports Illustrated* around."

"Oh! Well, I think we might. If not, I'm sure there are some *Good Housekeeping* in the living room," answered Aunt Leona.

"Come on, Cindy. Why don't you show me Leon's room," I said, changing the subject. Can you believe it? I mean, who wants to read *Good Housekeeping*?

Cindy led the way up the stairs to Leon's room, which was fine with me. She was really beautiful. When we finally got to the room, she pushed open the door, stepped aside holding her nose, and said, "Well, here it is. Welcome to Leon's answer to a Hollywood disaster film. We keep the door closed and the windows open year 'round because of the smell."

I stepped inside and eyed the room carefully. The bed looked made; that is, the spread had been pulled up over the pillows and covered anything that might be underneath. There was an old gym sock sticking rigidly out from the wall with no visible means of support. (That was a neat trick. I later learned that Leon had obtained a five-finger discount on a plaster foot from a shoe store display and mounted it on the wall of his room. It scared the hell out of his mother the first time she saw it because she had always told him this room was so bad his clothes could be stood up in the corner by themselves.) There were a few clothes scattered about (only enough for three or four days) to give the room that lived-in look. There were some records and books on the desk and dresser in no particular kind of order. And on the wall was a strange-looking calendar. The bottom half had the normal calendar for the month of June, but the top half had the face of a beautiful brunette above a rather large hole cut in the paper. "What is that?" I asked.

Cindy snickered and replied, "Oh, that! Leon bought himself a Playboy Calendar for Christmas and Mom blew a gasket. Dad compromised by cutting what Mother called the 'offensive parts' out of the calendar. Leon figured that what was left was better than nothing."

"Oh yeah!" I laughed. "What did Uncle Fred do with the 'offensive parts'?" She laughed too. Then changing the subject, I said, "Hey, Cindy, thanks for covering up about the gum. Frieda sure is a brat. How do you put up with her?"

"I don't know," sighed Cindy, "but every time I try to give it back to her, I catch it from Mom or Dad. I was sure glad to see you stick it to her today." I laughed. She paused a moment then giggled. "I don't believe I said that." We both laughed. "Anyway, maybe you can give her some of her own medicine while you're here. If there is any way I can help, just let me know. This could be a really fun week."

"Yeah," I grinned mischievously, "this could be fun. I'm already getting some ideas. Let's get together after supper and see what we can do." I figured, what the heck, Cindy was really neat. I might as well build up some points. After all, she wasn't blood-related to me. Plus, she might be visiting me some time and I've got some friends back home who'd try to sell New Testaments in a kibbutz for a chance to date her.

She left to go back downstairs. Half way down, she stopped and looked back. "By the way, the bathroom is at the end of the hall. The new-looking towels are for you. See you later." She winked, turned, and continued down the stairs, her soft blond curls bouncing as she descended. I sighed. Just then, Leon came bounding up the stairs with my suitcase in one hand and a guitar case in the other. He was a little taller than me. He looked to be about six-two or six-three. Since I'm five-seven when I'm fishing, almost everyone is a "little taller" than me. Leon had brown wavy hair just like Uncle Fred except he had a little more of it and it wasn't as neatly combed. It looked like he was trying to grow a moustache, but I couldn't tell for sure. He was also thin like Uncle Fred. He was wearing jeans that looked like they had come over on the Mayflower and a T-shirt that said, "TAKE A GOOD LOOK AND…" on the front and "…EAT YOUR HEART OUT!" on the back. He obviously had self-esteem issues. On each foot he wore what looked like half a tennis shoe.

"Hey, Joey boy," he called out. "How ya doin'?" He saw me looking toward the stairs past him. "She is cute, isn't she?" Then changing the subject, he said, "Sorry I missed you at the train station, but I had a guitar lesson. We got a folk group together at school and we want to sound real professional by fall. We figure we can cash in on the folk music craze. You know, the Kingston Trio, Limeliters, and Brothers Four all rolled into one. Hey, it's been two years since I seen ya. Whatcha been doin'?"

I felt completely intimidated. He was taller than me, he was cooler than me, he played the guitar, and he was in a folk group. All I'd ever done was play the piano (for six years) and I quit that when I found out that nobody played piano in the marching band. Now I had to come up with something impressive.

"Well, Leon, to be honest, not much. I got letters in football, basketball, and track this year and I'm an assistant manager at a drug store where I worked last summer. I start next week." Almost all of these statements were distant relatives to the truth. Actually, the football letter was for being team manager and the basketball letter arrived by mail and said basically that I shouldn't bother to try out for the team. The track letter, however, was legitimate though I had just barely earned the minimum number of points. As for being assistant manager in the drug store, well, I was a combination soda jerk and janitor. My employer liked everyone to have a title so in his store he was the owner, there was a manager, and everyone else was an assistant manager. He did draw the line when I asked to be referred to as a custodial engineer.

"Wow!" exclaimed Leon. "I'll bet you're just like your dad. He was really good in sports too. It's hard to believe since he's so small. 'Course, so are you. About the only team I could have made was girls softball but I couldn't pass the physical."

I laughed. Good, I thought, he was impressed. I'd better change the subject fast, before I get caught. "I'll bet there's lots to do in Chicago. I'm really looking forward to the night life. I mean, Benton Harbor is so dead. About all there is to do is wait in long lines to ride its only horse."

"Huh! Ride its only horse? I don't get it."

"You know what I mean. It's a one-horse town."

"Ooooohh! Hey, that's pretty good. Taking turns riding the horse. Tell that one to my old man. I'll bet he gets a hernia laughing. Actually, there is a lot we can do. Usually I don't get to go out a whole lot. My folks say one night a week is enough. Hopefully they'll let us go out every night while you're here. By the way, tonight I thought we might go to a White Sox game. They're playing the Yankees in a night game at Comiskey Park. I also got dates for us for tomorrow night. We'll go to a movie and McDonalds after. How does that sound?"

I'd never been to a major league baseball game. Already the week seemed to be off to a good start. I wasn't too thrilled about a blind date tomorrow night, however. I'd had four blind dates and blindness would have helped on three of them. "Sounds great," I said. "Tell me about this McDonalds place. I've heard a few things about it but I've never seen one."

"Oh, some guy saw a place out in California a couple of years ago. They sold cheap hamburgers, french fries, shakes, and soft drinks. He bought them out and started building them all over. I think their headquarters are on the south side somewhere. Anyway, there's a bunch of them in Chicago now. They just built one about a mile from here. They're not too bad and the girls love them. It's the only place I know where you can feed and water a girl for less than a dollar." Leon spoke with the confident authority known only to high school seniors-elect. Now he changed the subject. "We got a couple of hours before supper. Let's go out and shoot baskets."

"Sounds good," I said, "but I think it'll be more sporting if we use a .22 or a pellet gun rather than a shotgun. It gives the baskets a better chance."

"Very funny," replied Leon. "Let's see how good you really are. Play you a few games of HORSE. How about the best of seven?"

"You're on." I put my bag in a semi-occupied corner of the room, changed to my sneakers, and we departed to do battle in the driveway. Leon won in four straight but I managed to fake a mild ankle injury in hopes of covering my complete lack of talent. Mercifully, Aunt Leona called us to wash up for supper before any further damage was done to my pride.

CHAPTER 3

The First of Many Schemes

After supper, I went to the family room to watch a little TV before we left for the ball game. There wasn't much on but news and even that was a rerun, but it gave me a chance to talk to Cindy. We were alone since it was Frieda's turn to dry dishes while Aunt Leona washed. Uncle Fred was reading the newspaper in the living room and Leon was upstairs changing clothes. We began to scheme against Frieda.

"I need to know what Frieda does by habit and preferably away from the house. That way, when I do something neither of us will get blamed."

Cindy thought for a moment and then said, "I know. Every night she rides her bike to Walgreen's a couple of blocks from here and buys a candy bar. She also spends about fifteen minutes looking through the comic books while she eats it. If Mother knew, she'd kill her. Frieda's already put our dentist's son through two years of college. I haven't told on her yet because I hope to blackmail her sometime with it."

"Great!" I said. "Maybe I'll ask her to write a will and leave me her gold fillings. How far is the nearest gas station?"

"It's only two blocks," said Cindy. "Oh! But it's two blocks east and the drug store is almost three blocks west. Are you thinking what I'm thinking?"

"I'll bet I am," I replied. "Just make sure you are obviously around the house after Leon and I leave."

We left the house to go to the ball game just a few minutes after Frieda snuck out to the drug store to get her candy. I had asked him to take me to the nearest card shop so I could get a birthday card for my sister. Cindy had told me the card shop was next to Walgreen's and there was a parking lot out back. She said that she thought Frieda always parked her bike in front.

Leon was privileged enough to drive the "old" car. It was a 1954 two-tone Plymouth with a strange transmission called Hi-drive. You could drive it like a stick shift or just leave it in third, ignore the clutch, and drive it like it was an automatic. Of course, it clearly wasn't an automatic. It had all the get-up-and-go of a paraplegic tortoise. But it was better than taking the bus.

"You don't even drag race bicycles in this thing," he said as we pulled out of the driveway. "With ideas like this, I doubt Chrysler can last ten more years. If it were up to me, I'd be driving a hot little baby-blue '57 Chevy."

"Same here," I said. "But at least you can have some fun with the novelty of this one. You'd be amazed at what I have to drive. We've got a little Simca and I swear it's got a rebuilt Briggs and Stratton engine in it. My dad says it gets great mileage so he likes it. About all I can do when somebody pulls up beside me is raise a white flag."

"Yeah, I know what you mean," snorted Leon. "But you're right about having some fun with this one. We got a kid in our class named Homer Sweet. No kidding—that's his name. Anyway, one day I gave Homer a ride home in this crate. Now Homer is about the most gullible person you'd ever want to meet. So all the way home I drove like it was a stick shift. He tells me that he thinks a stick is neat and that's what he drives. Well, once we stopped at a light and I forgot to put in the clutch and shift. When the light changed, I pulled away and he was sitting there with his mouth just hanging open. 'How'd you do that?' he sez. Then I realized what had happened and I decided to really give him a good story. I looked at the odometer and it said something like sixty-seven thousand miles so I told him you could do that with any stick shift when there's a seven anywhere on the odometer. Well, he bought that line completely. A week later he was out with this chick named Lou Anne Meyer. Until she went out with Homer, I thought she was both cute *and* smart. Anyway, he was driving his dad's '55 Chevy with a stick shift and it just turned fifty-seven thousand miles. All of a sudden he remembers what I told him. So he decides to really be cool. He leans back and reaches over to put his arm around Lou Anne. Now Lou Anne usually only goes out with guys who drive stick shift cars so they won't put their arm around her when they're driving. She made some remark about him needing that arm to shift. He tells her that it's no problem 'cause his odometer just turned a seven in the thousands column so he won't have to shift for a couple of months. She figured he was crazy. As soon as they reach a light, he applied the brakes and started drumming casually on the steering wheel with his fingers. All of a sudden the car started jolting back and forth and the motor died. Old Homer couldn't believe it so he tried again at the next light, with the same result. By this time he was in too deep to just give up so he stopped at one of those high-priced, all-night service stations and tried to explain his problem. He told the mechanic all about the sevens on the odometer and the car becoming an automatic and all that. Well, the mechanic started laughing so hard tears were streaming down his face. Lou Anne just kind of curled up into a ball over by the passenger door and tried to disappear. Homer ran off to the rest room and stayed there for about twenty minutes. Finally he came out and took Lou Anne home. He never said a word to her. Can you believe a guy would do anything so dumb?"

As a matter of fact I could. He probably would have fooled me with that story. I don't think I'd have carried it as far as Homer though. But I could never admit that to anyone. That wouldn't be cool. "Gee, that sure was dumb," I said. "We've got a few slow ones back home, but nothing like that." I wanted to change the subject. "How do the girls react to this car when you have a date?"

"Oh, that's no problem." said Leon. "This is one liability that I've turned into an asset. I just make them believe that this kind of transmission is something really special. I tell them that it's experimental and Chrysler pays my dad to test-drive it. I mean, they'll never see another one anyway. I tell them it's the best of both worlds. It's both a stick and an automatic. Usually they beg me to let them drive it. I can usually make a fair exchange."

"Jeez, I guess I better be careful and listen to what you're saying," I said. "Do you ever tell the truth?"

"Only when there's nothing better," chortled Leon. "Well, here we are at the card shop. Let's park around back in the lot. I'll just wait for you."

"Thanks," I said, "I'll only be a minute." I quickly entered the card shop, picked up the first cheap card I saw (it was a Bar Mitzvah card), and paid for it as well as a stamp. Then I went out through the front door. Frieda's bike was parked right next to the front door of the Walgreen's store. I knelt down beside the bike and quickly let the air out of both tires. Then I went back through the card shop to the back parking lot and got back into the car. Leon pulled out and we headed for the ball game.

"Have you got a pen in the car?" I asked. "I'll mail this card if there's a mailbox between the parking lot and Comiskey."

"Look in the glove box. I think there's one in there. And I know there's a mailbox on the corner next to the parking lot near Comiskey."

"Thanks," I said. I retrieved the pen and quickly filled out the card. I signed it MOSES and addressed it to the ambassador, c/o the Saudi Arabian Embassy, Washington, D.C. I figured he probably didn't get many Bar Mitzvah cards from plain old average Americans. I carefully wiped off any fingerprints, just in case (good grief, now I'm saying it), and sealed the envelope. You never know how fussy Washington might be. From that point on, I handled the card only on the edges until I dropped it in the mailbox.

CHAPTER 4

My First Major League Game

We passed through the turnstile at Comiskey Park about twenty minutes before game time, plenty of time to get a snack before searching out our bleacher seats. We were both a little hungry after our light supper of four pieces of chicken, two baked potatoes, and three ears of corn on the cob (each), which we washed down with six glasses of milk (each). There hadn't been time for dessert. We decided it was about time.

We each carried a cardboard tray holding three hot dogs, two bags of New Era potato chips, and two of the largest cups of Coke they sold. Two catsup stains and one pop[1] spill later, we arrived at our seats and had gotten comfortable just in time to see the managers exchange the starting line-ups and batting order. The game would begin soon.

There was a special thrill I experienced that night. For the first time I was going to see some of baseball's greatest personalities in action. Casey Stengel was the manager of the Yankees and had put them in every World Series I could remember up to last year. The Yankees had

---

[1] pop: Midwest expression equivalent to the Eastern term "soda" and, in many parts of the South, "coke," which means any carbonated soft drink. In the Midwest, Coke means Coca Cola, Pepsi means Pepsi Cola, RC, means RC Cola, etc.

won most of them too. Al Lopez was the manager of the White Sox. They had won last year's pennant but had lost the Series to the Dodgers four games to two. There were high hopes that they would repeat as pennant winners and win the World Series this year. The Yankees had players like Mickey Mantle, Yogi Berra, Clete Boyer, Elston Howard, Bill "Moose" Skowron, Roger Maris, and Whitey Ford. The White Sox crew included Nellie Fox, Luis Aparicio, Sherm Lollar, Minnie Minoso, and Billy Pierce. I hoped one of the White Sox would hit a home run because the scoreboard at Comiskey was well known for going completely berserk when the home team hit a round tripper.

We all stood as they played the national anthem. Most people just stood quietly looking in the general direction of the flag, but some took more or less active roles. One older man a few seats away stood at rigid attention with his right hand to his forehead in a military salute. Another guy, two rows in front of us, was tall and thin and looked to be about fifty. He didn't bother to stand, probably because he couldn't. His eyes were barely open and he smelled heavily of cheap wine. Every once in a while he would open his eyes wide, give a big toothless grin, shout "Play ball!" and then go back to sleep. Right next to us on our right was a big, barrel-chested man in his early fifties who had been loud and raucous with his friends sitting with him before the national anthem. All during the anthem he cried quietly. Just behind us was a younger man dressed in a gray pin-striped suit who was singing loudly in a rich tenor voice with entirely too much vibrato. At first I thought he might be some important celebrity brought in for that purpose, but if that was true, I couldn't figure why they stuck him in the bleachers. I asked Leon, "Who is that guy? Is he a celebrity or something?"

"Not really," said Leon. "He's been at every game I've ever gone to, though. I think he just likes to sing. I heard he's a frustrated choir teacher at one of the Catholic boy's schools on the south side."

The preliminaries over, we seated ourselves and awaited the start of the game. The umpire yelled "Play ball!" and almost simultaneously the drunk opened his eyes wide, rekindled his toothless grin, growled "Play ball!" and returned to his stupor. The White Sox took the field and I squinted to see the faces that belonged to the more familiar names. Minnie Minoso was easy, not because he was black, but because I had so frequently seen him pictured in the papers with his signature wide, toothy grin. He was a crowd pleaser. The fans over in left field could be heard yelling "Hey, Minnie" as he jogged out. He acknowledged the crowd with a wave and that famous grin. Luis Aparicio and Nellie Fox were in the infield catching grounders and throwing them to Roy Sievers at first base. Billy Pierce was the starting pitcher. The first man he would face was Bobby Richardson, the Yankee second-baseman.

Not much happened until the second inning. Elston Howard, the Yankee catcher, had singled and Clete Boyer was at the plate. He parked the ball in the seats and the Yankees led 2–0. If a White Sox player had hit the homer, the score board would have gone spastic. A homer by the visitors was met with no such hoopla. But the Yankees were ready as we were treated to their answer to the Bill Veeck scoreboard show. Casey Stengel led the Yankees out of the dugout and they paraded around, each carrying a sparkler and whooping it up. Yogi Berra led a second contingent in like manner from the Yankee bull pen. At first the fans were caught off-guard by this unusual display, but soon there was a resounding Bronx cheer followed by echoes of "Yankees go home!" All of a sudden, I heard a resounding "Play ball!" from nearby. It was the resident drunk again, and by the time I looked over at him, he was asleep again. Everyone in our section was laughing by this time. Actually, from that point on, the Yankees were never in any serious trouble. Minnie Minoso scored for Chicago on an error by Boyer in the fourth inning. The Yankee pitcher, Art Ditmar, drove in Clete Boyer in the seventh and Mantle homered for New York in the eighth after which the Yankees repeated their antics of the second inning. It was much less effective this time. Even the drunk held his peace. The White Sox tried to rally in the ninth but could manage only one run. The Yankees won 4–2. There would be no celebrating on the South Side tonight. Still, I had enjoyed the game because of both the action that had taken place and the personalities that were involved.

As we were making our way out of the bleacher section, I tried to take notice of the people around us who had attracted my attention during the national anthem. The drunk was now sprawled across one of the planks that made up the bleacher seats. The old man who had stood at attention and saluted was now walking proudly up the steps toward the exit ramp. Though he moved with a measured, military-like gait, I couldn't help but notice the limp and the shiney metal of the brace attached to his left shoe.

The big, barrel-chested man was involved in very animated conversation with his two companions. "If it hadn't been for the Korean War," he said, "my two boys would probably be playing for the Sox. Tommy, he was the pitcher. Pierce isn't half the pitcher my Tommy'd be. If Tommy was here, Pierce would be picking fruit in Texas. You know what I'm saying?"

"Yeah, Chet," said one of his companions. "Tommy and Eddie were cracker jack ballplayers. Too bad about…" I couldn't hear them anymore.

I looked for the singer in the gray suit. I didn't see him. I listened carefully and didn't hear him either. But then, what White Sox fan would be singing after they lost?

"Well, Joey," said Leon, "at least there was a little excitement here tonight. Too bad the White Sox couldn't show you how to beat the Yankees, but…"

"That's OK, Leon. I really didn't care that much about who won. It was really neat to see a major league ball game. I had a great time just watching the people. You know the show on TV called *The Naked City* where they say something like 'This is the Big City. There are nine million stories here. This is just one of them.' Well, after tonight I think I can better understand what they mean. I wonder how many of those stories go completely unheard and unnoticed."

"Really getting philosophical tonight, aren't you?" chided Leon. "To be honest, I never really noticed. I guess when it's around you all the time, you just kind of ignore it." There was a short pause. Then he said, "All that thinking has made me kind of hungry. How about you? We haven't had anything to eat since the seventh inning."

"Yeah. You know, I could go for a Roxie burger. We've got this place back in Benton Harbor called Roxie's. They serve a gigantic hamburger for thirty-five cents and is it good!"

"Hey, we got something like that on the way home. It's called Big Patty's. That sounds good to me, too. Besides we might see some girls there. Let's go," said Leon enthusiastically.

CHAPTER 5

Big Patty's, Fawn, and Melissa

When we pulled into the parking lot at Big Patty's, there were cars parked, cars semi-parked, cars cruising, and cars pulled in at every one of the drive-in service ports. We found a spot in the back of the parking lot. "It's better to eat inside anyway," said Leon. "There's a better chance of meeting chicks who don't have dates. The only ones who use the drive-in ports are those who already have a date or those who aren't looking." That would never have occurred to me.

As we entered, there were two guys leaving. They wore leather jackets (it must have been eighty degrees out), smelled like junk-yard dogs, had their hair all slicked back and wore long sideburns. They were smoking Pall Malls and trying to act drunk for some incomprehensible reason. They probably hadn't had anything stronger than cherry cokes. Inside, most of the clientele was more civil-looking. There were tables of guys, tables of girls, and tables of guys and girls. We found an empty booth and slid in. Judging by the smell and the cigarette butts, the booth had just been vacated by the two leather jackets. The waitress came over and quickly cleaned up. Then she sprayed some room deodorizer around and apologized for the smell. In a raspy voice she said, "Pedro and Linus. Those are the two guys you passed on the way in. They come in here every night, order two cherry cokes, then sit here, smoke, sweat in those jackets, and stink up the place. Sorry about the smell. Al, he's the manager, makes us spray the booth when they leave. He must have tried a dozen different sprays before he found one that worked. This is the best so far. It's lilac. How do you like it?" Her tag said her name was Patty. She was probably nineteen or twenty and kind of plain looking but also cute in a way. Her hair was a non-descript brown and worn in a poodle cut. She had a cute smile, a nose that was a little too big for her face, wide-set hazel eyes, and razor-thin eye brows. She was about five-two, average weight, and had a figure that wasn't bad but really didn't do anything for me. I think it was the single hair growing on the side of her nose that caused me to rate her a C-minus rather than a C.

Leon spoke first. "Well, Patty, I'll tell you. The lilac isn't great, but it's an improvement over the Pedro and Linus residual bouquet. That perfume you're wearing is better though. Why don't you spray a little of that around?"

"Oh, that," she said. "That's Shalimar. The perfume, I mean. But I don't have any here. You'll have to settle for the lilac. And my name is Sue, not Patty. Al makes all the girls wear that name because that's the name of the joint. We put our collective foot down when he wanted the name tags to say Big Patty. Now, what can I get you?"

"Let's have two Big Patties with everything, two french fries, and two large cherry cokes," said Leon. "How about it, Joey?"

"Sounds good, Leon. I think I'll have the same," I said. Patty, or Sue, or whoever she was, rushed off with our order. Leon and I started to look around to see if there were any unattached girls who could pass inspection. Most of the best-looking girls had dates. Isn't that always the way it is? There were two booths and a table of just girls but they looked like they were waiting to be registered by the American Kennel Club. Then we saw them. Over in the corner booth were three great-looking chicks. "Hey, Leon," I said, "do you see those three over there? They look like they're all A-plus to me."

"Yeah," said Leon, "but there's two of us and three of them."

"OK, so we'll flip a coin to see who gets two. What's the problem?"

"It doesn't work that way," said Leon patiently. "They just get real defensive and figure that if there's only two guys, one of them is going to get left out. They probably won't even talk to us."

"Well, we could try. What have we got to lose? They don't know us anyway," I offered.

"OK, Romeo. You go over and talk to them. I'll follow you," countered Leon.

"They're Chicago girls, Leon. You have more experience and understand them better. You go first and I'll follow you." I was starting to chicken out. Leon probably knew what he was talking about.

"I'm telling you, it won't work. The numbers are all wrong," said Leon with a note of finality.

"Yeah. You're probably right." I sighed. "Our food will be here soon anyway." Just then, a tall guy and a short guy went over to the corner booth and started talking to the three girls.

"They don't have a chance. Just watch," said Leon.

I did watch. After about thirty seconds, one of the girls got out of the booth, the short guy slid in, and the girl got back in. Now the short guy was between the two prettiest girls. The tall guy sat down next to the girl on the other side of the booth. They made some introductions and seemed to be getting on very well. I looked at Leon. Leon was counting ceiling tiles.

Our food arrived, for Leon a reprieve from the kitchen. Somehow Sue had managed it all in one trip, including straws, napkins, and extra catsup. Everything was good. The Big Patty was every bit as big as the hamburgers at Roxie's. The bun was about eight inches across with sesame seeds all over the top and the hamburger stuck out all the way around.

We had each started our second hamburger when Leon nudged me under the table with his foot and nodded over toward one of the AKC tables. Two girls had gotten up and left and the other two were headed toward our booth. They both were wearing light blue shorts with white blouses and sandals. One was so skinny that the only things that bulged on her were knee and elbow joints. She had long, straight black hair separated into neat falls on either side of her face, which was symmetrically divided by one long and two short, perfectly horizontal lines of her mouth and eyes and the vertical line of her nose. She was a walking stick person. The other one was her complement. She was all bulges. Her legs were like tree trunks but indented at the knees. From there up, things got worse. When she let her arms hang down, they stuck out away from her body at a thirty-degree angle. From shoulder to fingertip, there was a natural taper from gigantic to merely large. Above her fourth chin was a cavernous mouth surrounded by walnut-sized cheeks. Her eyes were buried deep in her face below bushy, bleached eyebrows. Her hair, rust colored with white-blond streaks, was mercifully tied back in a bun. She emitted a continuous giggle.

"Hi, fellas," she gurgled. "You look lonely. We thought we'd cheer you up. I'm Fawn and this is Melissa." She sat down next to Leon the Lucky. I felt the booth lurch. The skinny one sat down next to me. As she did, I looked closely. The line of her mouth grew but remained straight. I think she was smiling.

I was speechless. Fortunately Leon wasn't. He was prepared. "Hi, ladies. I am very pleased that you were concerned about us, but really, we are fine. This is Brother Jonathan and I am Brother Simon. We are studying at St. Anthony's Seminary in Waukegan and hope to be ordained in just six more years. In fact, we will be going to the Ozarks next week to spend our summer working among the poor. Perhaps you would keep our humble efforts in your prayers?" He sure was convincing. I was ready to go home and pack.

"Gosh, we didn't know." Giggled Fawn. "I hope we didn't offend you. We'll pray for your work, right, Melissa? Well, we really should be going." As they got up to leave, the table did a reverse lurch. The thin line of Melissa's mouth lengthened. I think she smiled again. I realized that she had not said a single word. It was like this pair needed to be together just to balance things out.

"Think nothing of it, ladies." Leon was too much. "We are truly flattered." They quickly made their way out the door. I could never have pulled that off. In fact, I caught myself wondering what would have happened if I had been with someone more docile than me instead of with Leon.

We finished our food. We each left a quarter tip. This was the first time I had ever been in a situation where I should leave a tip. As we paid our bill, I observed to Leon, "The prices are pretty good. A buck seventy-five each isn't bad. I think that's about what it would be at Roxie's and the cokes are bigger here."

"Yeah. It really is pretty reasonable." said Leon as we went out the door. "Whaddaya say we have a banana split when we get home? I think Mom has everything we need in the house."

"I've always got room for a banana split," I said. "You're on." I looked back through the window to see what was happening at the booth with the two guys and the three girls. It looked like the short guy was getting phone numbers from *both* of the girls he sat between. Could that have been me? It was too painful to think about.

CHAPTER 6

Frieda Cooks Breakfast

Saturday morning rolled around all too soon. It was, however, a mixed blessing. At least I wouldn't have to listen to Leon snore. His adenoids must be a testimony to the theory of survival of the fittest. Why they hadn't ruptured by now, I'll never know. I don't know about the rest of him, but his adenoids were in superb shape.

Leon was awakened by Aunt Leona's bright, cheery voice reminding him that he had promised to wash the car before she went shopping. I was already awake. Leon had seen to that. Leon sat up, threw his legs over the side of the bed, stretched, yawned, and shook his head vigorously. (I was to find that this was a ritual with Leon.) "OK, Mom," he said. "I'll be right down." He got up and started to dress. I did the same. I decided not to comment on his snoring. After all, I was a guest and it just wasn't right to complain about things like that. Besides, he could deny it. He couldn't hear it; he was asleep.

"Well, Joey, how'd you sleep?" Leon almost sounded like he cared.

"Fine, Leon. How about you?" I asked as though I didn't know.

"All right, I guess." He paused. "Hey, Joey, did you know that you snore something awful? I think you cracked the plaster on the ceiling."

So much for being Mr. Nice Guy. Next time I'll shoot first and ask questions after. "Gee, Leon, I'm sorry. I guess I just wasn't listening.

I have a tendency not to when I sleep." Good grief. How can I change the subject? I decided to just keep quiet and get dressed. Car washing meant jeans, a T-shirt, and sneakers, or maybe just going barefoot. Leon was similarly dressed. As we started to leave the room, I looked back and noticed the unmade bed. "Don't you have to make your bed?" I asked. According to my mother, every child in America over five and still living at home was bound by civil law to make their bed.

"Oh sure!" said Leon. "But I figure if I never do it without being told, maybe they'll give up. Besides, you're company. Maybe they'll let it slide."

"Leon!" It was Aunt Leona from her bedroom. "Don't forget to make your bed before you go downstairs."

"OK, Mom," hollered Leon. Then quietly to me he said, "Do you believe it? She must be psychopathic."

"You mean 'telepathic' don't you?" I asked.

"Oh? Oh yeah. I guess that is what I mean. You go ahead downstairs and I'll be down in a minute."

I walked down the hallway. Cindy's door opened just as I was about to pass it. "Oh, hi!" said Cindy. "Joey, watch out for Frieda today. She was really mad when she came in last night. I think she's suspicious. I heard her mumble your name a few times on her way upstairs. She got grounded for today because she didn't get home on time last night. Do you think she saw you?"

"Not a chance. Anyway, what could she do to me?" I said. Cindy sure looked great. She was barefoot, wearing jeans and an old plaid long-sleeved shirt tied just above her waist with the sleeves rolled up. Her blond hair was neatly combed and pulled back into a pony-tail that had a soft, bouncy spring to it. I'm a real connoisseur of pony-tails, and Cindy in a pony-tail was an A-plus. I decided to let her walk ahead of me. It never hurts to be polite.

"Just the same, be on your guard. She's ingenious when it comes to making trouble."

We proceeded downstairs and went to the kitchen. Leon arrived just behind us. Uncle Fred was sitting at the table reading the morning paper and Frieda was at the stove. "Morning, boys," said Uncle Fred. "Frieda's making breakfast today. How do you want your eggs?"

"I'll have mine over easy and don't break the yolk, sis," said Leon.

"I'll have mine scrambled and break the yolks on mine," I said.

"Oh, Joey. You are so clever," mocked Frieda. "How about you, Cindy?"

I'll have them scrambled, same as Joey," replied Cindy. We sat down around the kitchen table. As we waited for breakfast, Leon looked through the entertainment pages for a movie to see that night. Meanwhile, I explained the rules of "salt shakers" to Cindy. Salt shakers was a nifty little game we played in the cafeteria at school during lunch hour. It was really quite simple. All you needed was a regulation salt shaker (glass, wide-based, and tapering to a narrow head) and a table with a smooth surface and smooth vertical edges. The idea was to slide the salt shaker across the table so that the base protruded over the edge of the table without falling off. For close calls, a stiff card was slowly pushed up the edge of the table. If there was any contact with the salt shaker, it was good for a point. Usually the game was played until one player had ten points, or the salt shaker broke, or the Gestapo stopped the game.

Cindy was just starting to get the hang of it when breakfast(?) arrived. The table settings were early Woolworth plates, cups, saucers, and gas station give-away aluminum juice cups. I recognized it immediately because we had a very similar set at home. My mother figured that people were least functional and thus more accident-prone during the first two hours after awakening. If they were going to break anything at our house at breakfast, at least it would be cheap and easily replaced. Besides that, the plates looked so bad anything on them had to look good.

Clearly, this line of thinking would find a worthy patron in Cook Frieda. I must admit, she gave the plates a good run for the money. My plate had a blue flower print on a scorched white surface. The edge showed signs of having melted at least once. On the plate was a runny pile of scrambled eggs, which had a gray-brown hue and two very black sausage links inadequately protected by two wedges of very lightly toasted Wonder Bread, which appeared to have been assaulted and mutilated by a crazed Visigoth armed with a butter knife and rock-hard butter. There was slight evidence that some butter had actually been transferred to the toast during the attack. My purple aluminum cup contained a dark liquid, which appeared to be helpless. Someone was sure to comment on this gastronomical monstrosity but it wasn't going to be me.

It turned out that Uncle Fred took up the gauntlet. "Well, Frieda, what kind of juice do we have today?" Clearly he was using a diplomatic approach.

"It's grape juice, Dad," said Frieda proudly. "How does the rest of it look?" A courageous question. Smart? Maybe not.

"I'm sure it will taste good," replied Uncle Fred hopefully.

I figured that at least the juice should be safe, and since I liked grape juice, I gulped it right down. That habit would have to change. Mine was not grape juice. It was prune juice. The little brat was striking back.

"Oh yuck!" Cindy's mouth was contorted in reaction to the eggs. "What did you do to the eggs, Frieda?"

"I scrambled them, just like you asked," Frieda said defiantly.

"Well, what did you add go them? They taste really strange," said Cindy suspiciously.

"Like always, I added a little salt, pepper, and milk," replied Frieda defensively.

"But Frieda." This time it was Aunt Leona. "I thought we were out of milk. Where did you find any?"

"Oh, we had a little chocolate milk left from early in the week. I just skimmed the skin off the top and used that." Frieda was really trying to sound innocent.

"Well, that's just awful! Joey and Cindy, you don't have to eat them," exclaimed Aunt Leona.

It was too late. I tend to eat eggs really quick while they're still hot. I had just gulped the last of them down when I caught the reference to curdled chocolate milk. I now had a weird sensation that the eggs might not be with me long. I was still hungry but afraid to try anything else. She had already booby-trapped me at both ends. I was determined to have my revenge. The wheels were starting to turn. As we left the table, Cindy suggested that we meet after she finished the dishes. Since Leon and I would be washing the car, she said she would help me clean out the inside of the car and we could talk then. She agreed that something had to be done about Frieda.

CHAPTER 7

Washing the Car

Leon and I decided to do the job on the car just like it's done downtown. We would wash and wax the car and do a thorough job of cleaning the inside. This wasn't because Aunt Leona was going shopping; it was to impress our dates tonight. Leon was taking out his almost steady girlfriend and he swore on his Gibson steel string guitar that my date was also a knockout, though not as cute as his girl. I took that to mean that either she was beautiful or that she was as interesting as a coma. I would find out tonight. At least her name sounded interesting. It was Erica Andersen. Leon had told me the story about his "almost" steady girlfriend. Her name was Phyllis Yockey. Leon had been going out with her for almost three months but her parents wouldn't let her go steady. This meant she was supposed to go out with other guys if she was asked. She hadn't been asked out by anyone else in the three months he had been dating her. (I wondered why, if she was as cute as he indicated.) It also meant that he should go out with other girls. He usually didn't but he did make good use of most opportunities to do some girl-watching and flirting, which did occasionally lead to a date.

In fact, we were going to the beach tomorrow afternoon for that very purpose. Leon said Sunday afternoon was a good time for his favorite pastime since most parents stayed away from the beach on Sunday because it was so crowded with teenagers. Most teenagers, both male and female, went to the beach for exactly the same reason: to be seen by the opposite sex. I wonder what parents do for fun. I mean, I can't imagine anything more entertaining than a large crowd of teenagers.

We set to work on the car, first washing the exterior, then drying it with a chamois. We had just started to apply the wax when Cindy came out to help me clean the interior. Once inside the car, even with the windows down, I began to notice how warm it was. The heat plus breakfast was beginning to churn my insides. On top of that, Cindy was wearing perfume. Now I've got nothing against perfume, and Cindy's perfume under other circumstances (sans the evil breakfast) would have had a very different effect, but at this point, I was beginning to feel sick. I was now even more determined to strike back at Frieda, this time with a vengeance.

"We've got to think of something truly devastating this time," I said. "I feel like I may be sick most of the day from that gastronomical horror this morning. Did you know that she gave me prune juice, not grape juice?"

"She didn't! Why that little bi—" she caught herself, "brat. What are we going to do?" Now Cindy was doing her best to stifle a laugh. I could tell that this news struck her as both tragic and funny. I suppose it would be if it weren't happening to me.

"I've got something cooked up for later in the week, but it will be too obvious who did it. I'll set it up so that I'll be on my way home before the trap is sprung. Right now we have to come up with something that will look like it is entirely her fault and make her look dumb either at home or in front of her friends. By the way, does she have any friends? I may be assuming too much here."

"Oh yeah, she has friends, and they're all delinquents just like her." I could tell Cindy was really fond of Frieda's friends.

"Tell me, Cindy, is Frieda a packrat? You know what I mean. My sister always brings home stuff she collects during the day. You never know what she will bring home. And she always leaves it scattered around the house. Is Frieda like that?" I asked.

"She sure is. What she usually picks up are items from restaurants. You know, napkins, straws, those little packets of sugar or catsup or mustard, things like that. Mom is always complaining about finding them in her pockets when she does laundry."

"Good. Now, what usually happens when she has to go to bed, especially on the weekend?"

"Oh, she always puts up a fuss. In fact, tonight she will probably put up a huge fuss because when she is grounded she usually has to go to bed early and she really hates that, especially on the weekend," Cindy replied.

"Great. Now, one more thing. What is her room like? Does she make her bed?" The wheels were turning now.

"It's almost as bad as Leon's room, and I know she didn't make her bed today. I guess Mom was just too tired to fight with her. Say, just what do you have in mind?"

I explained it to Cindy. She was absolutely delighted.

CHAPTER 8

The Blind Date

I could not believe how nervous I was. Supper was like the last meal before an execution. There was plenty of food and it was good, but I just couldn't get serious about eating. It seemed silly to get so uneasy about a blind date but I was nonetheless. As I went upstairs to change I hoped that the prune juice had finished its work and my insides would calm down for the rest of the evening. The thought of being stuck with an ugly and/or completely uninteresting date for possibly the rest of the week was most disconcerting. The way I read the odds, there was a 95 percent chance that I would get a total loser, a 4 percent chance that the situation would be neutral, and a 1 percent chance that I would meet the love of my life (or at least the love of my week).

Since this was Phyllis's friend and Phyllis was Leon's girl, I had to appear to be at least mildly interested. If I didn't, Phyllis would probably get mad at Leon and that could really louse up the rest of the week. I vowed to myself that if things worked out badly, I would invite Leon to visit me for a week and fix him up with Judy Boshke.

Judy was an almost pretty girl, until you had been with her for fifteen minutes. She was a chain smoker (I already knew that Leon couldn't stand girls who smoked any more than I could), she couldn't say more than eight consecutive words without including a profanity or vulgarity that would starch your collar, and she had a small but very noticeable Marine Corps tattoo just above the sleeve line of a short-sleeved blouse. You could catch a glimpse of the tattoo every so often when an arm movement caused the sleeve to ride up her arm momentarily. The normal reaction was, "Did I see what I thought I just saw?" She also had a stopwatch in her brain. The minute she got you in a car, she would start necking.

The priest at school had told us some things about dating and one of those things he emphasized was that it was okay to kiss provided you followed a few rules. The rules were simple: 1) no kiss could last longer than ten seconds, 2) both mouths must remain closed during the kiss, 3) there should be at least four minutes between kisses, and 4) there should be no more than four kisses in one hour or nine kisses in one day. I'm not sure how he arrived at the numbers and I have never seen them anywhere else, but from then on these were considered gospel by the girls of the school in general and enforced to the letter by Judy Boshke in particular.

Judy's kisses lasted exactly ten seconds (at least according to Dale Hillman who actually borrowed a real stopwatch to carry out a "scientific study") and she always initiated them in safe situations (in front of her house, at a stoplight, etc.) and only after the usual disclaimer that she was a good girl and you had better not try anything funny ("funny" wasn't what the guys she dated had in mind). Actually the guys who went out with her were so familiar with the routine that they were too busy mentally counting (one-Mississippi, two-Mississippi, three-Mississippi, etc.) to think about trying anything funny.

Guys I knew who had been out with her verified that she followed all the rules exactly. Her kisses never exceeded ten seconds (nor were they less than that), her mouth was always closed and you got slapped if yours wasn't, you always got exactly four kisses per hour with at least four minutes in between and if you could last more than two hours on a date with her, you got exactly nine kisses for the evening. The last one was delivered on her doorstep. Ten seconds after it started, the porch light went on and she opened the door and went inside. Even her parents bought into the ten-second rule. To her credit, she never asked if you had kissed anyone else that day, nor did she cut you short if she had kissed somebody else.

I certainly hoped that there was no Judy Boshke in my future. From what Leon told me about Erica, it seemed I was saved from that fate at least. I guess I was as ready as I could be. I put on my bravest smile and went downstairs to meet Leon and drive off to my fate. On my way through the living room, I passed Cindy who was reading the newspaper. I gave her the thumbs-up sign and winked as I went by. She smiled and winked back, knowing that I had just set the trap in Frieda's room. "By the way," she said, "enjoy your blind date. I think you'll have a good time. Erica is really nice."

There it was. I was doomed for sure. Cindy had used the word "nice," which every guy understands to mean "a good personality, at least by girls standards, but not really all that much to look at." My stomach started rumbling again.

Leon was in the family room watching the end of a Cisco Kid rerun on TV. We went out to the car (freshly waxed outside and squeaky clean inside) and began our drive to Phyllis's house. "Kinda nervous aren't you, Joey? How come?" asked Leon. When I get nervous, I tend to bounce my knee up and down. In this case, I had both knees going. I guess it was pretty obvious.

"Yeah, I guess I am. I suppose it's the uncertainty of tonight. I really don't know what to expect and I don't want to mess things up for you," I said.

"Oh, don't worry about that. Phyllis and I already worked that out. If you don't like Erica, just be sure you don't say anything about how long you'll be here or about going bowling on Tuesday night. We'll fix you up with someone else for Tuesday if tonight doesn't work out. You probably should know that Erica has some of the same concerns. You're being scouted too, Joey. She's not going to ask how long you're staying in Chicago unless she's interested. If you two want to get together, I figure you'll find a way. Now relax. Just try to have fun." Leon seemed very reassuring. Maybe I would spare him from a date with Judy Boshke. However I think I was more nervous than ever. It never occurred to me that I might be less than phenomenal as a date. Good grief!

Mercifully the suspense was nearing an end. We pulled into a driveway in a subdivision about fifteen minutes from Leon's house. Phyllis's house must have been designed and built by the same person that did Leon's subdivision. I couldn't believe the similarity. We went up to the door and Leon knocked. Phyllis's father (I presumed) opened the door and greeted us with a friendly handshake. Leon introduced me to Mr. Yockey and his wife who was just behind him. Casually, we were guided into the living room where two girls were seated on a maroon couch.

The next few seconds seemed to proceed in slow motion. I looked at the two girls as they slowly rose from the sofa and glided toward us. Immediately I knew who my date was. One girl could only be described as gorgeous. She was about five-three, nice figure, very pretty face, sparkling blue eyes, beautiful shoulder-length light brown hair, and a smile that made Doris Day look constipated. She had to be Phyllis. The other girl wore a tan dress, was about five-six, a little chunky (big-boned?), average face, average hair, average smile and eye-glasses enclosed by substantial rims with calico cat ear pieces. Oh, well. If I didn't pass this test, I wouldn't worry about it. She was okay. Things could be worse, but then, things could be better too. I tried to give a convincing smile.

"Joey, this is Phyllis," said Leon as he introduced me to the average girl. Wait a minute! The average girl? That means…I couldn't believe it. I'm sure my smile brightened about 150 watts.

"It's nice to meet you, Phyllis," I said, trying to contain myself.

"And this is Erica Andersen. Erica, this is my cousin Joey Winters." Leon smiled knowingly to me, reached over, and took Phyllis's hand and moved toward the door.

Erica flashed a big smile and said, "Hi, Joey. I'm looking forward to the show." She gathered up her purse and a light sweater from the couch, put her arm through mine, and we followed Leon and Phyllis to the door.

"You kids have fun now. Nice to meet you, Joey," said Mr. Yockey.

"Enjoy the show!" added Mrs. Yockey.

As we walked to the car, Erica maintained a light hold on my arm. Not that I minded. I took it as a good sign. At least my appearance didn't revolt her. I was determined to show her the best "me" possible. I held the door open for her. As she got in, I noticed that Phyllis had gotten in and scooted over to the middle of the front seat. Immediately I was confronted with an awkward situation. When I got in the backseat with Erica, should I slide over close to her or just sit by the door? I was getting ready to close the door and go over to the other side when Erica said, "Come on, Joey. Get in on this side." She giggled lightly. "It'll help balance the car." Then as an afterthought she said "I learned that in physics class" and took my arm again as I got in.

So far, I hadn't said a word to her. I was getting worried. What should I say? Leon had gotten in on the driver's side and was backing the car out of the drive. We had about twenty minutes to the movie theater. We were supposed to see *The Greatest Show on Earth,* which was a movie about the circus.

Before I knew it, we were just talking as though we had known each other all our lives. I'm not quite sure how it happened, but it did. We first talked about physics class since I had also taken physics in my junior year. Erica took physics because she wanted to be either an aeronautical engineer or a science teacher. Then we talked about family, school, favorite TV shows (she also liked *Maverick*), and other pastimes. Very soon I was comfortable and Erica seemed relaxed and happy. She even laughed at some of my very small jokes. All of a sudden time seemed to be passing all too quickly. We were at the theater. Erica and I decided to share a box of spearmint gum drops (they were her favorite too) and we chose our seats moments before the show started. I decided to be cautious. I didn't want to do anything stupid or seem to be pushy so I didn't try to hold her hand or put my arm around her shoulder or anything like that. As we got into the movie, I realized why the girls had wanted to see it. One of the stars was Cornel Wilde who seemed to be the current heartthrob. He was a trapeze artist in the movie. At one point, he fell from the trapeze after having cut down the safety net. As he fell, Erica jumped in her seat and grabbed my hand with both of hers. I reached over with my other hand and returned some of the pressure. (Maybe I learned that in physics.) As the tension of the scene ebbed, so did the pressure of our mutual grip. I took one hand away as did she. She did not remove her other hand. She did adjust the grip slightly to be more comfortable for both of us. I don't remember the rest of the movie. I just remember that she didn't let go of my hand the rest of the evening.

CHAPTER 9

What? No Banana Split?

After the movie, we went to the nearest McDonald's and sat around eating hamburgers and fries and drinking vanilla shakes. The four of us talked for another hour. It was as though we had been a gang for years. Erica seemed to be enjoying herself, and I know I was having the most enjoyable date (blind date at that) of my life.

We finally left the McDonald's and got in the car for the ride home. In another half hour the evening would be drawing to a close. Again we were talking as we had on the trip to the theater. As we talked, she would release my hand to use her hand to draw a picture in the air or to otherwise emphasize a point, but each time she would reach back for my hand. We talked, we laughed, we gave and received the joy of each other's company. I felt suspended in time, separated from the past and the future and wishing for neither. Finally, now was important. I remember only the great sense of peace and comfort I felt. I remember none of the conversation until she asked, "How long will you be in Chicago, Joey?" Oh my gosh! There it was. *The question.*

"I leave next Friday," I said. I glanced up front at Leon and Phyllis. They both had a smirk that told volumes as they glanced at each other. Erica had looked up at them too and then looked quickly back to me. All of a sudden I was reminded that there was a future. I wanted to see her again. I was sure she wanted to see me again. No point in holding back. "I really do want to see you again, Erica. I think Leon was planning to take me bowling on Tuesday night. Could you go with me?"

"Tuesday would be great. I have to babysit my little brother tomorrow night and I have another sitting job on Monday but Tuesday is fine," replied Erica.

I finally figured it out. It was her smile that made the conversation with her so easy. I would never have thought I could fall in love with a smile, but now I knew I could.

"Say, why don't I call you tomorrow. By then I'll probably know what time Leon wants to go bowling on Tuesday." Of course Leon was right there. I could have just asked him. Obviously Leon was also aware of this. He started to open his mouth when Phyllis poked him in the ribs with her elbow. His mouth closed immediately. "Besides," I said, "I really enjoy talking to you." (Thanks, Phyllis.)

"I'd like that," said Erica. She released my hand and started to fumble around in her purse.

"What are you looking for?" I asked without thinking. Sometimes you don't want to know what they are looking for.

"Silly," she said. "If you're going to call me, you'll need my phone number. It's unlisted because we were getting a lot of crank calls." She withdrew a pen and a small piece of paper from her purse and began writing. "There. We're going to my aunt's for dinner tomorrow, but I should be home by seven. Call me after that."

She handed me the number, which I carefully placed in my wallet. I then reached for her hand, which I held in both of mine. It looked like she was about to say something when we turned into a driveway. "This is where I live," she said. "I'm only a few blocks from Phyllis's house."

I opened the door. Since I had to get out first anyway, I decided to walk her to the house. We took our time. Leon and Phyllis didn't seem to mind. They were snuggled close together in the front seat. The porch light was on but all the curtains were drawn. We stood there a moment looking at each other. Finally, Erica spoke. "I can't remember when I enjoyed an evening so much. Thank you, Joey." She squeezed my hand.

I squeezed her hand back. "Thank you, Erica," I said. "I feel the same way. I'll call you tomorrow night. And I'm really looking forward to Tuesday."

She released my hand, turned slowly, opened the door, and went in. "Good night, Joey," she said. Her smile was wonderful. It almost made me shiver.

"Good night, Erica," I said, smiling back. She closed the door. I floated to the car and got in. Leon and Phyllis quickly separated and Leon backed out of the driveway. I hardly noticed. I began to daydream.

The next thing I remember was being back at Leon's house, getting ready for bed and turning down a double banana split.

CHAPTER 10

The Morning after: Sunday Mass

The sun shone brightly through the window making it impossible to sleep any longer. I had slept really well; even Leon's snoring hadn't kept me awake. I feared waking up. I wasn't sure I wanted to separate dream from reality. Leon was already up and rummaging around the floor for something suitable to wear to church.

"Did we go to a movie last night?" I asked.
"Yeah," said Leon.
"Did I meet a girl named Erica last night?" I asked.
"Yeah," he said.
"Did I like her?" I continued.
"My guess is yes."
"Did she like me?"
"Definitely."
"Did I have fun last night?"
"Absolutely."
"Am I still dreaming?"
Leon slugged me on the arm. "Did you feel that?" he asked.
"Oowww! Yeah, I felt it," I said, rubbing my sore arm.

"Then you are not dreaming, Joey," he said. "All that stuff really happened."

"That's a relief." I grabbed my wallet and opened it expectantly. I found the slip of paper Erica had used to give me her phone number. If I'd thought of that first, I wouldn't have gotten punched on the arm. Live and learn. "Well, what's on the schedule for today, Leon?" I started to dress.

"Okay, first there's breakfast," he said. I winced. "Then we go to Mass at noon. Dad calls it the Gary Cooper Mass. Then we have dinner after mass and then we go to the beach. After that, I don't know. Maybe we'll get lucky at the beach."

"What does Uncle Fred mean by the Gary Cooper Mass?" I asked, not really awake yet.

"Oh, you know. The Mass at High Noon," he answered.

"Oh yeah. My dad calls it the Mass of the Hung-over Faithful because most of the late arrivals as well as the last four rows seem to usually be in that state."

"It's not that way here. We have a one o'clock Mass for them. That pretty much insures that the noon Mass will not be longer than about forty-five minutes. Come on, let's go to breakfast. Don't worry, Frieda probably isn't cooking today," said Leon, noticing the apprehensive look on my face.

I had just finished dressing. I felt a little hungry, probably because I had passed up the double banana split last night. The others were already gathered around the breakfast table. I looked carefully about. Nobody was cooking. There was juice and coffee on the table along with a plate of donuts. This time I could see through my juice glass. Inside was what appeared to be orange juice. Today was already starting out better than yesterday.

Now if it could just end as well. Uncle Fred was again reading the paper, this time the sports section. Aunt Leona was looking through the TV section. Frieda was nibbling on a donut with a severe pout on her face, and Cindy was trying her best to contain her glee as she winked at me. At first I couldn't figure out why. Then I remembered the booby trap I set for Frieda last night. Everybody was quiet and I saw no reason to try to change it. I sat down with Leon and ate a couple of donuts and drank a glass of orange juice followed by two glasses of milk. Then since it was her turn, I offered to help Cindy with the breakfast dishes, seeing as how there weren't very many anyway.

"Oh, you don't need to do that," said Aunt Leona. "By the way, did you have a good time last night, Joey?"

"We had a great time. It went about as well as you could expect for a first date," I answered. "And I really don't mind helping Cindy. It's the least I can do, seeing as how you're so good to have me over for a week."

"Why, that's nice of you, Joey. Isn't it, Fred? We'll just go out to the living room so you can clean up. Frieda, you get down to the basement and do that laundry." Aunt Leona got up and followed Uncle Fred and Leon out to the living room. Frieda stomped down the basement steps. Cindy broke out in a stifled but hysterical laugh.

"It went perfectly, Joey. When Mom sent her up to bed early because of Friday night, Frieda went up, changed to her pajamas, and then came back down and tried to talk her way out of the punishment. Of course it didn't work and she stormed upstairs again and took a flying leap into her bed. Then she started pounding and jumping around and then she screamed. By the time she figured out what was happening, she was covered with a mixture of catsup, mustard, and sugar, all from those packets you put in her bed. She looked a sight. Mom was furious. She made her wash the sheets and pajamas by hand and then soak them overnight in bleach. Now she has to do all the laundry for the next three days. She tried to blame you and me for it, but her room was such a mess that Mom didn't believe her. I couldn't wait to tell you about it." She gave me a big hug. What could I do? I hugged her back. I felt a little strange about enjoying it. It was a brief hug and soon we were back to finishing up the dishes.

"Do you think she will be out of our hair now?" I asked.

"I doubt it. I think it's her nature to be a pain," Cindy answered as she wiped the table and counters. "By the way, how did your date with Erica go?"

"We had a really good time. She's real nice. I'm supposed to call her tonight. We will probably go bowling Tuesday. Do you know her?" I inquired.

"I know who she is. We've talked casually a couple of times. She seems real nice. She is a grade ahead of me at school and she's a really good student. She will probably graduate as the class valedictorian," said Cindy. "If you're calling her tonight, be careful. Frieda likes to listen in on the phone, and from what I hear, Erica's brother, I think his name is Glenn, likes to listen in too."

"Oh, that's just great. Tell me, if I give Frieda a handful of Preparation H, will she disappear?" I said despairingly.

Cindy laughed. "I never thought of that, but I'd say it's worth a try."

"Oh, also, do Glenn and Frieda know each other?" I asked.

"Sure they do. They are in the same class at school. She says she can't stand him because he's always pushing her in line and calls her 'Fraidy Cat Frieda.'"

"Hey, that's great. I think I'm ready for them to listen in. Just let 'em try," I said with a note of anticipation.

"Someday, Joey, I'm going to find out how that mind of yours works. I wish I knew what you were talking about," said Cindy.

After we finished the dishes, Cindy and I played gin rummy until it was time to go to church.

The six of us arrived at St. Ursula's Church at ten minutes before twelve. We had a good choice of seats with the church being about half filled at that point. Aunt Leona led the way to an empty pew about two-thirds of the way up the middle aisle. We filled our half of the pew, which had sort of a divider in the middle. The other end of the pew opened on the side aisle. The pew in front of us was occupied by a lone individual who was seated on the middle aisle side of the divider. I knew he was doomed, no matter where he sat in that pew.

I have found that there is a basic rule for those individuals who arrive early to a church service and try to occupy an empty pew. No matter where they sit, they will be asked to shift to one side or the other before services begin. If you sit on either end, a group of people looking for seats will seek you out and ask you to move down toward the center of the pew. If you sit in the middle of the pew, a group will come along that is large enough to force you to move to whichever end of the pew you had thought about parking in before you moved to the middle. It was just a matter of time before the poor fellow in front of us would have to move. He was obviously unfamiliar with the Law of Church Pew Displacement.

As we entered our pew, Leon seated himself, put down our kneeler, and then reached back and put down the kneeler of the pew behind us. Protestants never get to do this; it is a strictly Catholic symbol of manhood (having legs long enough to otherwise kick down the kneeler behind you) of which members of other religions were deprived. When we were growing up, all the boys eagerly awaited the day that their legs were long enough to have their feet touch the raised kneeler behind them and their arms were long enough to lower the kneeler behind them without straining.

Just before the service began, a family of nine chose the pew in front of us from the middle aisle and another natural law was upheld.

CHAPTER 11

Misadventure at the Beach

After Mass, we returned home and had a swell dinner of rump roast, mashed potatoes, gravy, asparagus, tossed salad, rolls, plenty of milk, and a dessert of coconut cream pie (one of my favorites). I was convinced that the meal would give us the energy for our trip to the beach. After dinner, we went up to get into our beach clothes, grab towels, and a small portable radio. We were starting down the stairs when we heard Cindy behind us. I looked back. She had on a modest but striking black-and-pink diagonal striped bathing suit. She was gorgeous. "Wait for me, guys."

"Oh no!" wailed Leon. "Mom, she can't come with us. She'll mess everything up."

"Leon, she just wants a ride to the beach and back. She said she wouldn't bother you and Joey," said Aunt Leona.

"Oh, Mom! What if we meet a couple of girls there? She'll just be in the way. Come on, Mom, don't make me take her," pleaded Leon.

"Oh, Leon!" said Cindy. "If you meet any girls and you can actually get them to go out for a Coke, I'll take the bus home. Don't worry. I won't be in your way." She sure wouldn't be in my way. I didn't mind if she came with us.

"Now, Leon, you'll take your sister to the beach and that's that," said Aunt Leona with a note of finality.

"Okay!" said Leon. "But I won't be responsible for her. Once she gets there, she's on her own."

"That's fine with me," answered Cindy. "Let's go."

The three of us squeezed into the front seat of the Plymouth and drove to the beach. Cindy sat between Leon and me but sat closer to me in an attempt to stay as far as possible from Leon. Not that I was complaining. The drive was made in nearly complete silence with Leon visibly fuming. As we approached the beach parking lots, Cindy asked, "Do you have beaches like this where you live, Joey?"

"We sure do," I said. "In fact from here it looks just like the beaches on our side of the lake. Lots of sand and lots of people. The only difference is that the sun is in front of me at home and it's behind me here when I look at the water."

"I keep forgetting that you live on the other side of Lake Michigan," she said. I suppose it should be about the same." We had found a parking place and were getting out of the car. I kind of hoped Cindy would be riding home with us. "Well, guys, have a good time. When and where do you want me to meet you, Leon? I really do mean it. I'll take the bus if you want me to."

"You just be back here at six thirty. If we have dates, we'll drop you at a bus stop," said Leon. "Now, beat it."

"I'm gone," she said, running off carrying her towel and sun tan lotion. "Have fun, Joey."

"Bye, Cindy," I said. "Enjoy yourself."

Leon and I started walking toward the beach. It was huge. It seemed to stretch for miles in both directions. "Here's the plan," said Leon. "We'll find a place where there is a volleyball net and lots of girls by themselves. That combination is a sure winner." We walked about three hundred yards and found a spot similar to Leon's description. We put down our towels and radio and took off our sneakers. We couldn't decide whether to take a swim first or just rest on the towels and look over the prospects. We finally chose a swim.

The water was pleasant and just a little choppy, making for some energetic fun in the waves. We stayed in the water for a while, and though we saw several attractive girls, we could not come up with a plan for meeting them. You just don't meet girls while you are in the water. Finally, we went back to our towels and lay down to let the sun dry us.

At the nearby volleyball net, there were four girls trying to play volleyball. The ball got away from them and landed inches from my face, kicking up some sand. As I sat up to brush the sand off my face, one girl approached to get the ball. "I'm sorry. Hey, why don't you guys join our game? The more people we have, the more fun it is." She seemed sincere, and more importantly, she was kind of cute. So were the others.

"Sure!" said Leon. "We'll be right over." She ran back to the net and waited, talking animatedly with her friends and looking over at us. "See, Joey. I knew this would work. This is great luck. We get a choice. There are four of them and they invited us."

We got up and walked over to the girls. Up close it was too good to be true. There were three blondes and a brunette. All were quite cute. They were also friendly and energetic. "Hi!" I said. "I'm Joey and this is Leon. What are your names?"

The brunette, the one who had retrieved the ball, spoke. "Hi. My name's Ginny, and this is Amy, Beth, and Betsy," she said as she pointed out each. "Why don't you guys choose up teams?"

That certainly was one way to get things started. I was giving serious thought to moving to Chicago. I had never had this much luck in Benton Harbor.

"Go ahead, Joey," said Leon. "You choose first."

"Okay. I'll take these four," I said, pointing in the general direction of the four girls. "Now you pick, Leon." The girls giggled.

Ginny spoke up. "Aawww, Joey. That's not fair. I think when you pointed over here, you pointed to me first so I'll be your first pick. Now you pick, Leon."

Actually she was right. She would have been my first pick so this was working out well.

"I'll take Amy, then," said Leon. Of the group, she was probably the prettiest. I wouldn't have chosen her first because she seemed a little bit aloof. I also got the impression that she thought she was the prettiest. Anyway, I like brunettes. "Go ahead, Joey, your pick."

Beth and Betsy were about equal in appearance. Quietly I asked Ginny, "Which one is the best volleyball player?" Based on what I had seen before the ball landed next to my face, none of them was very good.

"I don't know," she said. "This is the first time any of us has played. Why don't you take Beth? She's always the last one to get picked. It'll make her feel good not to be last."

Then it occurred to me. This wasn't about winning a volleyball game. It was about having fun and the best way to do that was to treat everyone with a degree of respect. "We'll take Beth," I said. I was happy with the choice and I was even happier that Ginny trusted me to make the choice given what she had told me.

Beth came over to our side of the net and Amy and Betsy went with Leon to the other side. We began the game with only slightly more success than the girls experienced before we joined them. I had to keep in mind that volleyball was not our primary objective. I assumed the same held true for the girls. After just a few minutes, four guys came by and asked if they could join in. "Sure!" said Amy. And now there were ten.

It wasn't long before we were joined by several more girls and another crowd of guys. Things went on like this for about an hour until finally there were, at my last count, eighteen boys and sixteen girls. Apparently volleyball was not meant to be played with seventeen-person teams. The game broke up when one of the guys (who already had made his choice of girls) suggested that everyone go for a swim. It was like musical chairs. Every guy tried to grab the hand of one of the girls and run to the water. Sixteen guys were successful. Leon and I were not. I kept looking around for Ginny. I finally spotted her at the water's edge being carried into the lake by a guy big enough to be a linebacker for the Bears. She seemed happy enough. Leon and I looked at each other and shrugged. We picked up our towels and trudged off toward the next volleyball net feeling we had picked up some pointers at the last game. We decided we would be the ones to suggest going for a swim as soon as we had chosen a companion. Off we went, scarred but not defeated.

At six-thirty we returned to the Plymouth dragging our towels. Now we were defeated. Rule number two: another person's plan will not work for you. On top of that, we were sunburned. As we approached the car, we saw Cindy (definitely not sunburned) standing next to some guy who looked like Paul Anka. "Hi, guys," she said. "This is Larry Sanders. He's going to give me a ride home. We're going to stop at McDonald's first. Tell Mom I'll be home by eight-thirty." And off she went with Larry.

Leon was really steaming now. "We go to all this work and she just tags along. Then she ends up with a date. That stinks!"

"Oh, don't worry about it, Leon. I had a good time. You've got to admit that we did stay busy and we met a lot of people. I've already had more luck in three days here than I would have in three months at home. I'm tired. Let's go home." We climbed into the car and found our way home. Leon's dreams for the day may have been dashed but I still had a phone call to make.

CHAPTER 12

Frieda and Glenn Pay the Price

While the others were watching TV, I dialed Erica's number. I was using the phone in the den, which, I was told, was more private. I felt a bit anxious and quite nervous. Erica seemed like a nice person and I didn't want to do something stupid that would cause her not to like me. Her phone rang three times before she answered. "Hello, Andersens' residence."

I recognized her voice. "Hi, Erica. This is Joey," I said.

"Hi, Joey. I was hoping it would be you," she said enthusiastically.

"Good. I talked to Leon and he said we would be going bowling about seven-thirty on Tuesday. Can you go? I sure hope you can." I was afraid that I sounded too desperate.

"I asked my folks as soon as I got home last night. They said I could go. I'm looking forward to it." Erica sounded happy.

"That's perfect. You know, I really enjoyed our date last night. I'm almost ashamed to say it, but I wasn't expecting much. I haven't had much luck with blind dates. You sure changed that." I was starting to relax. Maybe I was relaxing too much. I usually keep my feelings to myself. There was something about Erica that made me want to be more honest and open. It was frightening.

"I know what you mean. The few blind dates I've been on were not very good either. I figured that at least I was doing Phyllis and Leon a favor so they could go out. All of those negative feelings evaporated when I got to know you last night. Even my brother Glenn couldn't ruin my day today. I've just been waiting for your call. By the way, speaking of Glenn, if you hear a click, it's probably him listening in. He does it all the time." She didn't seem terribly annoyed even at Glenn. Maybe she really liked me.

"Yeah. Cindy was telling me that Frieda does the same thing. If you hear a second click, it's probably her. I'm ready for it, though. If you hear the clicks, just follow my lead." I used my most mischievous tone.

"That sounds like fun," said Erica. "Not to change the subject, but I've never asked a guy out before. A friend of mine is having a small pool party on Thursday evening and I was wondering if you would go with me? My friend said I could invite Leon and Phyllis too. There will be four or five couples. And her parents will be home. I couldn't go if they weren't."

"I'd love to go. I'll find some way to go even if Leon can't. I'll talk to Leon later about it. That will give me an excuse to call you again tomorrow," I said. There was a click. Was it Glenn or Frieda?

"I like the way you think. If Leon can't go, and if you don't mind having a girl pick you up for a date, I think I might be able to get the car," she said. There was another click. Now both Frieda and Glenn were listening in. It was time for me to go for the kill.

"That would be fine with me. I don't care who drives. I'll just be glad to be with you. I was wondering, do you think Glenn would like to come along and take Frieda to the party? I understand Frieda has a big crush on Glenn." I heard a gasp that was quickly stifled. So this is what a conference call is like.

"It's funny you should mention it. Glenn has a thing for Frieda too. I'll have to look into that. Maybe they could go with us." Erica had picked up the lead beautifully. There was another stifled gasp, followed by two sharp clicks. The eavesdroppers had hung up.

"Joey, that was ingenious. They can't do anything about it either. If they complain to their parents, they'll get punished for listening in.

It was a perfect set-up. Gosh, Joey, I really like you." Erica sounded sincere. I was beginning to feel like I did after our date last night.

"I like you a lot too, Erica," I said with honest abandon. "I'm really looking forward to Tuesday, and I'll call you tomorrow evening and let you know about Thursday. Can you give me the number where you'll be babysitting tomorrow?" She gave me the number and we said our good-byes. I went into the family room to watch TV with the others. I couldn't wait to tell Cindy what Erica and I had done to Frieda and Glenn. I just knew she would love it.

CHAPTER 13

Stop and Smell the Roses

I woke up Monday with the same smile on my face that I had when I went to sleep the night before. At least that is what Leon told me. It was the kind of smile that you feel all over. I suspect that my thoughts of Erica were responsible. Today was going to be a great day. It had to be. All day I would be looking forward to talking to Erica that evening. Also, Leon had a pretty interesting schedule lined up for us. The highlight seemed to be that I would be meeting a friend of his named George "Mad Dog" Norkus. Leon assured me that Mad Dog would live up to his name. This sounded pretty interesting. In addition, I would have the opportunity to see Leon's folk group rehearse. That evening, we would be listening to the Patterson-Johansson rematch for the heavyweight championship. Add to that the phone call to Erica and a good day becomes a great day. It was the kind of day that reminded me of something my grandmother used to say. "On your way to watching a spectacular sunset, don't forget to stop and smell the roses." This was her expansion of the old admonition to stop and smell the roses. Talking to Erica tonight would be my "spectacular sunset," but it looked like Leon had planted a few roses for me to stop and smell along the way. I reminded myself to try to stay in the present.

This time I had slept more peacefully. Apparently Leon had stopped snoring. At least he must have quieted down quite a bit because he didn't bother me. We had talked the night before about the pool party Erica had invited us to attend. Leon said that he would not be able to go because his folk group had its first job that night singing at some little kid's birthday party. Apparently the kid wanted the Kingston Trio. The kid's parents knew Uncle Fred and Aunt Leona and also knew that Leon's group did some of the Kingston Trio songs. I guess the kid bought it because his parents were paying Leon's group fifteen dollars to sing for thirty minutes. Leon was planning to take Phyllis to watch the performance and then they were going out with the other guys in the group for pizza. That would blow the fifteen bucks and probably a little more. I was originally going to go along with them until the pool party with Erica came up. I guess I would have to tell Erica that we'd be using plan B. I could live with it.

We were about halfway down the stairs when I heard Cindy approaching from behind. As I think about it, I'm not sure how I knew it was Cindy and not Frieda. I guess I was already getting accustomed to the sound of her step. It was too gentle to be Frieda and too light to be either Uncle Fred or Aunt Leona. I turned to look at her. As usual, she looked fresh, a little different than yesterday (I think she did something a little different with her hair), and cute as usual. "Hi, guys," she said. "Gee, Leon, your snoring was absolutely devastating last night. You cracked some plaster all the way down in my room. You better see a doctor." Then she looked at me and smiled. "Joey, I don't know how you got any sleep. Why don't you tell me your secret?" She seemed to sense that I had good news about Frieda. (Good news for Cindy, bad news for Frieda.) Leon just gave a gesture of disgust, mumbled "I don't snore," and continued on down to the kitchen while I stopped to talk to Cindy. I wasn't sure whether she was kidding about Leon snoring or not. If she wasn't, I may have made a break-through medical discovery: A smile caused by a pretty girl makes you deaf to snoring.

"Cindy, you are not going to believe this," I said excitedly. I was anxious to share what had happened last night during the phone call to Erica. "I was talking to Erica when we heard a click followed by a second click. I knew they were both on the phone listening in. I suggested to Erica that Frieda had a crush on Glenn and maybe we could get them to double with us on Thursday. Then Erica, playing along, said that she knew that Glenn really liked Frieda. You would not believe the reaction. They knew they couldn't say anything but they quickly hung up. I'll bet they won't be able to face each other for weeks." By now, Cindy was sitting on the stairs and nearly hysterical with laughter.

"I'll have to make sure that they get plenty of chances to be near one another. It'll be fun to watch them squirm. I think I'm beginning to understand what justice and irony mean. I guess it's always better to learn about justice when it's applied to someone else," she said as she stood back up and put her hand on my shoulder, rested her head on my arm, and continued to laugh. We resumed our descent down the stairs and joined the rest of the family for breakfast. Frieda's face turned bright crimson when I looked at her and winked. Cindy could hardly contain herself.

CHAPTER 14

Mad Dog

After breakfast and a brief clean-up job in the kitchen, Leon and I went off to meet Mad Dog Norkus and a couple of other neighborhood friends. Our plans were to play basketball at the schoolyard courts a few blocks from Leon's house. We first picked up Ken Peters, Marc Jefferson, and Skip Lewis, all friends of Leon living within two blocks of Leon's house. Another block away was Mad Dog's house. It looked pretty normal. Our knock at the door was answered by a short kid in a yellow T-shirt who looked a little like a fire hydrant. This apparently was the famous Mad Dog Norkus. He seemed a bit soft spoken and reasonably well mannered. He even asked his mother if he could go out and play basketball with some friends. Of course, he was already on his way out the door when he asked, and if his mother said anything other than yes, nobody heard it. I couldn't stand the suspense. I had to ask, "How did Mad Dog get his nickname?"

You'll find out in a few minutes," said Skip. "Come on, guys. Let's go by old man Shaker's place on the way to the courts." We headed north, back toward Leon's house. About a block before Leon's house, we turned east, and as we approached a corner lot with a fenced-in yard, I noticed that Mad Dog's confidence seemed to build and he began to stick his chest out a little further with each step. As we got closer to the house, I saw a large bulldog roaming freely in the yard and a sign on the fence that read BEWARE OF DOG. Mad Dog moved out ahead of the rest of us and then started to act very strange. First he got down on his hands and knees. Then he started to growl and drool at the mouth. Next he made some loud barking noises. It didn't take much to get the bulldog's attention and Mad Dog certainly had the dog's attention. The dog was at the fence barking furiously. Mad Dog continued to make noise and then, suddenly, he charged the fence still on all-fours. He was really growling now. When he reached the fence, he jumped at it and sounded like a watchdog on a tight leash just inches from an intruder. The bulldog retreated, still barking but with much less conviction. Mad Dog kept up his act and seemed to get more convincing by the second. Finally the bulldog ran for the cover of his doghouse. Just as the dog reached safety, the front door of the house opened. Out stepped an old man with a big stick in his hand. Mad Dog just kept up the act. The old man started shouting. "What are you doing out there? Get out of here. Damn kids. Get out. You're giving assholes a bad name."

With the last comment, we all started laughing. Even Mad Dog gave up his act and returned laughing to where we were standing. Apparently the old man did not want us standing there laughing at him and his dog. He started hobbling down the steps toward us, stick in hand. We turned and ran off. As we rounded the corner, I could see a hand-made sign attached to the back of the BEWARE OF DOG sign. It said BEWARE OF IDIOT. Apparently this was a warning to the dog. It seemed a good time to turn our energies to playing basketball. Ken was the first one to comment on what was apparently a regular occurrence in the neighborhood. "Well, he did it again," said Ken. "Every week old man Shaker comes up with a new insult to hurl at us. He must work on them over the weekend."

"Yeah," said Marc. "I still remember the times when we made more than one stop in a week. We got the same insult. I wonder if he only expects us to stop once a week."

"I'm not sure he wants us to stop," said Leon, "but his comments sure can be colorful. They usually make our efforts worth the trouble. By the way, what was the gem he came up with last week?"

"How could you forget?" said Mad Dog. "He said that if a man-eating tiger attacked us we'd be safe but the tiger would starve to death."

"You mean you guys do this sort of thing to Mr. Shaker every week?" I asked. "How did that get started?"

"We've been doing it since last summer and we only do it during summer vacation," said Mad Dog. "It kind of started by accident. We were walking by his house one day on our way to the school yard to shoot baskets and Ken was drinking a bottle of pop. The bottle slipped out of Ken's hand and broke on the sidewalk just as old man Shaker came out the door. He just let out with one of his funny insults and told us to clean up the glass. While we were cleaning up the glass, the dog stood at the fence and barked at us. That's when I got the idea of striking back. I've been perfecting my routine ever since. The insult cracked us up so much that we just kept stopping every week or so since then. He has never disappointed us. We like him though. In fact, we shovel the snow from his walk and driveway all winter."

This was certainly an interesting neighborhood. There was something likeable about the old man. It was good to know that he wasn't bent on doing us bodily harm. And then there was Mad Dog. Talk about strange. I could think of only one kid back home that even approached the zaniness of Mad Dog and that was Lumpy Furgeson. Lumpy was a fighter; not a very good one, but a fighter nevertheless. He was always talking his way into a fight and then losing the fight. He had been beat up so often that his lumps had lumps. That's how he got his name. Lumpy was just crazy. Mad Dog was clever crazy. Lumpy would have done the same thing Mad Dog had done even if there was not a fence between himself and the bulldog. Lumpy would have lost that one too.

CHAPTER 15

The Basketball Game

When we arrived at the school yard there were already four other guys there playing basketball. Ken and Marc knew them pretty well so we got together and chose up teams. The new guys were Al, Nick, Ben, and Zeke. I never did catch their last names. Ken and Zeke were captains and I was the last one chosen on Ken's team. That was probably because I was both short and an unknown quantity. Mad Dog was the last one picked on Zeke's team and I hoped that I would at least be able to out-play him.

The team I was on consisted of Ken, Leon, Ben, Marc, and me. We were the shirts. Zeke's team was the skins. (I knew there would never be true equality between male sports and female sports as long as we could play shirts and skins.) With Leon we had the height advantage. The other team with Mad Dog had the big mouth advantage. We decided to play full-court. That meant a lot of running back and forth. I think the other team was hoping that Leon would get tired and we would lose our height advantage. By virtue of a coin toss, we got the ball out of bounds first. Being the shortest, I was elected to be point guard.

We played mostly a run-and-shoot style of ball. On our first possession I took the ball down the court and to the left side of the free-throw lane. Leon was an easy target so I passed high to him and he faked left, then took a step to the right and sank a hook shot. That seemed easy.

Then it started. Mad Dog began a steady chatter that was sometimes loud and shrill and other times almost a whisper. He was their point guard. On their first trip down court, all ran except Mad Dog. He just kind of shuffled down the court as though the ten-second rule had been suspended. As he approached the top of the free-throw circle he tried to fake left and go right. Everything went to the right except the ball and me. I grabbed the abandoned sphere and ran alone back to our end of the court and made an easy lay-up. We were ahead 4–0.

On his next trip up the court, Mad Dog, continuing his steady stream of nonsense chatter, reached mid-court, and stopped. He wound up and fired the ball at the basket. It went in. "Great shot, Mad Dog. Absolutely superior." That was Mad Dog's self-evaluation. The chatter never stopped and never made any sense.

On our next possession I took a jump shot from the top of the free throw circle and made it. I suspect I was more surprised than anyone else. Nobody else (with the possible exception of Leon) knew that I was a terrible basketball player. I was starting to get some confidence.

On Mad Dog's next trip down the court, I stole the ball from him and again went in for an easy lay-up. At this point, Mad Dog, still chattering like a wind-up toy on a tight spring, decided that it was too much effort to keep running back and forth so he just stayed down at his team's end of the court. Our team soon had a sixteen-point lead. I was hitting shots I had never thought of taking before. On top of that, I was making some pretty fancy passes to my teammates.

Zeke's team started to make a comeback by letting Mad Dog do all the talking but keeping the ball away from him. Mad Dog didn't appear to mind. He seemed to recognize that the best conditioned part of his anatomy was his mouth. He was pretty comical standing alone down at one end of the court, shooting invisible balls into non-existent baskets and the whole time keeping up a steady line of babble. It was a relatively short game. We won 204–162.

After the game, we stopped at a neighborhood ice cream shop. The sign on the door read: "THE SUNDAE SHOPPE, Closed Sunday, Open Mon.–Sat. 9 to 9." Inside we made straight for the pop cooler. We each got two twelve-ounce bottles of lime (green) pop. We were each given a Coke glass with crushed ice and a napkin. All this cost us thirty cents each. We all sat on stools at the long counter. The place was mostly occupied by teenagers drinking bottled pop from glasses generously filled with crushed ice.

At one of the tables there was a mother with two young children. They were sharing a banana split. They were expensive. They cost sixty-five cents. Apparently we were still sweating. When we sat down a few of the kids who were at the counter before us got up and moved to a booth.

Twenty-four ounces of lime pop later we left THE SUNDAE SHOPPE and went our separate ways. Leon and I headed back home for lunch, a shower, and then it would be on to the folk group rehearsal.

CHAPTER 16

The Folk Group Rehearsal

Having showered and then polished off two hamburgers each and a one-pound bag of potato chips along with a half gallon of milk, we were ready to rehearse. At least Leon was ready to rehearse. I was just going to watch. Not that I minded. I like folk music, and if these guys were any good at all, I would certainly enjoy the rehearsal.

We arrived at Frank Potter's house only a few minutes before Ernie Jakes, the third member of the trio. When everyone had arrived, we went down to Frank's basement rec room. The first order of business was to christen the group with a name.

"We have a job for this Thursday night and we don't have a name," said Leon. "Come on, guys, this is embarrassing. These people asked me what the name of the group was and I had to tell them we were still working on that."

"Hey Leon," said Frank, "what is this about a job? I don't know anything about it. Do you really think we're ready?"

"Yeah Leon," chimed in Ernie, who seemed the most nervous member of the group. "I don't know if we should try to go public yet. I really don't think we're ready. We need a lot more rehearsal. Besides, we only know four songs. What kind of a job can we get with just four songs?" Then, as an afterthought, Ernie added, "How much will we get paid for this job?" It appeared that monetary considerations might cure Ernie's nervousness.

"Look, guys, it's a job, but it's not a job," said Leon. "What I mean is that these people my parents know want us to sing for their kid's birthday party."

"Oh great!" sighed Frank. "A kid's birthday party. We don't have to dress up as clowns, do we?"

"There is no way I'll dress up as a clown and sing," said Ernie emphatically. "And I'm not serving cake and ice cream either. What have you gotten us into, Leon?"

"Relax guys," countered Leon. "No costumes and no serving. All we have to do is sing for thirty minutes and they will pay us fifteen dollars. The rest of the evening is ours. I figured we could go out for pizza and celebrate our first professional job. Come on, fellas. We can fill in the thirty minutes with four songs and jokes. You know that all the groups talk a lot and tell jokes between songs. We could even learn a new song today. That would make five."

"Right, Leon," said Frank sarcastically. "We know more songs than jokes. Besides, the only jokes we know are ones we've heard a hundred times already. You saw the Limeliters with us last spring. Their jokes were all new. Where are we going to come up with new jokes?"

"I dunno," said Ernie thoughtfully. "We would be getting fifteen dollars. Maybe we could learn two new songs. Then we wouldn't need as many jokes. Besides, between us we must know somebody that's funny and could make up a few jokes for us. What about Mad Dog, Leon? He's a pretty funny guy."

"Oh, he's funny all right," said Leon caustically. "But he's funny acting, not funny talking. Do one of you guys want to act like a rabid dog in front of an audience?"

"All right. So Mad Dog was a poor choice," admitted Ernie. "How about Lloyd Brewster? He's always got funny stories to tell. Of course we would have to take out all the dirty words. That would reduce it by half, but he is funny."

"You might have something there," said Frank. "Do you guys remember any of Lloyd's stories? Let's see if we can make it presentable. How about the one he told us about his Uncle Willard and the trip to Las Vegas?"

"No chance. The funniest part of that story was what happened to Uncle Willard when a prostitute approached him in the casino just after he had spilled his drink all over himself." Leon reminded them. "You can't tell that story to a bunch of eight-year-old kids."

"Yeah, you're right," admitted Frank. "Hey! I just thought of something. Remember the story he told about his brother Floyd and the roommate who bought a sweatshirt? We could act that one out. It was clean and I'll bet we could make it funny. There's a sweatshirt over on the table. Let's see what we can do. Ernie, you be the roommate who buys the sweatshirt. Just bring it along with you and bring it out and put it on after the second song. Let's give it a try."

"Good idea!" said Leon, handing the shirt to Ernie. "Come on, Ernie. Start it off."

"Okay," said Ernie, assuming what he thought was the look of a cheerful but gullible college freshman. "Hey, guys. Look what I just bought. These were on sale over at the bookstore." Ernie proudly held up a baby-blue University of Chicago sweatshirt. "Let me try it on. Tell me how it looks." He quickly removed the shirt he was wearing and donned the sweatshirt.

"Looks great, Ernie," said Leon, giving Ernie an admiring but sharp slap on the back. "How much did you pay for it?"

"It was on sale for only two-fifty," boasted Ernie. "Why don't you go over and get one, Leon? You too, Frank."

"Sorry, Ernie," said Frank with a woeful tone. "There is no way I'm going to buy that color sweatshirt. Tell me, were they all that color?"

"Well, yeah, Frank. I think they were," said Ernie. "What's wrong with the color?"

"On the way over here I heard on the radio that the dye they use for that color sweatshirt comes from Japan and contains some radioactive uranium," warned Frank. "I'll tell you this, Ernie, I think the bookstore was just trying to unload them before the government catches up with them. If I were you, I'd take that shirt off. You aren't experiencing any mild burning sensations, are you?"

"As a matter of fact, I am," said Ernie, pointing to his back. He had obviously forgotten that Leon had slapped him on the back. Ernie quickly stripped off the sweatshirt and turned to have Frank and Leon look at his back.

"I don't like the looks of this," said Frank ominously.

"The looks of what?" asked Ernie nervously.

"Gee, Ernie. There's a big red spot on your back," observed Leon, looking at the spot where he had slapped Ernie earlier. "You better see a doctor after we finish here."

"Don't get too uptight about it, Ernie," said Frank. "It's probably just a temporary rash. Maybe the bookstore will give you your two-fifty back."

Ernie started to scratch his back and side. He quickly put on the shirt he had worn earlier. He certainly looked like a candidate for the Homer Sweet award. I must admit, it was a pretty good act.

"Well, Joey, what did you think of that? Was it funny? You did laugh, didn't you? I guess if you laughed it was funny." Now Ernie seemed genuinely nervous. During the skit he was acting. I could tell the difference.

"Yeah, Ernie. It was pretty funny. Now," I said, "if you can sing, find some way to fill in between the remaining songs, and come up with a name for your trio, you may be in business. And don't forget, if you count "Happy Birthday," then you know five songs."

"Okay, guys. That's one problem solved," said Leon. "Now let's come up with a name for our group. Does anyone have any ideas?"

"Let's consider the names of the groups who are big now," said Frank. "That would be the Kingston Trio, the Brothers Four, and the Limeliters. Now, what do those names have in common?"

"Absolutely nothing, Frank," said Ernie. "Does that help?"

"No, I guess it doesn't," admitted Frank.

"Wait a minute, guys!" said Leon. "It does help. It means we need to come up with our own name. A unique name. We can't try to copy someone else's name."

"Great," said Ernie. "That leaves out the Chicago Trio, the Friends Three, and the Spotliters. About the only thing left is the Aardvark's Assistants and I just don't think the world is ready for that."

"Maybe not," said Leon, "but I think we're on the right track. Let's get some paper and put down all of our ideas. How about the Bow Tie Trio? We could all wear bow ties."

"None of us knows how to tie a bow tie," answered Frank. "Maybe we should call ourselves the Klip-ons."

Suddenly names were flying from everyone. Offerings included "The Songbirds," "The Teen Idles (not a typo)," "Just Plain Folk," "Idiots'

Revenge" (Ernie couldn't quite seem to get the idea), "Three Bean Salad," "The Fifties Nifties," "The Frog's Croak" (Ernie again), "Klean Kut Kids or KKK," "The Chicks Delight," "The Trinomials," "The Shepherd's Flock," "The Colonels," "The Shipmates," "The Great Lakers," "The Mellow Tones," "Insomnia's Answer" (something had to be done about Ernie), "Twisted Sockets," "Two Tenors and a Fiver," "The Hippo's Tummy Tuck," "The Spinal Chords," and finally "ELF."

"ELF?" queried Frank. "Whose idea was that?"

"Mine," I said. "ELF stands for Ernie, Leon, and Frank. You can either use the word or the letters. It's innocent sounding and nobody else is using it."

"I kind of like it," said Leon.

"So do I," said Frank.

"Gee, guys. You didn't like any of my suggestions," whined Ernie. "Oh, well, I guess I can live with ELF."

"Great!" said Leon. "Now we need to rehearse. Let's get the instruments out and get started." Ernie and Leon each opened a guitar case and removed a guitar. Leon's was the standard Gibson with six steel strings. Ernie's was a twelve-string guitar, the first I had ever seen up close. Frank had two instruments. One was a guitar, which was smaller than Leon's and had nylon strings instead of steel. The other was a five-string banjo, again the first I'd ever seen. I had been fascinated by guitars and banjos as soon as the folk music craze began. I had always wanted to learn to play at least one or the other of these instruments. I hoped that the guys would be able to take a little time and teach me a few things.

They began tuning their instruments, each oblivious to what the others were doing. When they seemed satisfied that their instruments were properly tuned, they decided to strum a few cords together. The sound was awful. It was like a wind-chime shop in a hurricane. Even their faces twisted in agony. They were clearly not all blessed with perfect pitch. Since Frank, who appeared to be the thinker in the group, had used a pitch pipe, they decided to re-tune to his guitar. About ten minutes later, they seemed content with the sound. It was much improved. If tuning took fifteen minutes, they wouldn't need all of the four songs they knew for the birthday party.

"Okay, guys," said Frank. "We know four songs. Which one should we do first for the party?"

"I think we should start with 'Tom Dooley,'" said Ernie. "That always get things off to a good start."

"I think we should follow with 'This Land Is Your Land,'" added Leon. "Then we could do the sweatshirt skit as a lead-in to 'It Takes a Worried Man.'"

"Good idea, Leon," agreed Frank. "Of course that leaves us 'The MTA' as a closing number unless we can learn something new this afternoon. Any ideas?"

"I'd like to learn 'Scarlet Ribbons,'" said Leon. "That's always been a favorite of mine."

"Well, I'd like to do "With Her Head Tucked Underneath Her Arm,'" said Ernie.

"Good grief!" sighed Frank.

"I don't know that one, Frank," said Ernie.

"Barfing chickens!" exclaimed Leon.

"Okay!" capitulated Ernie. "So let's learn 'Scarlet Ribbons.' But Leon, promise me you'll do 'Barfing Chickens' for me sometime."

"Let's go through the four songs we know and the skit just like we will on Thursday," said Frank. "We can time it out and see if we need to learn a new song." Then as an afterthought, "Oh yeah, let's add in 'Happy Birthday.' What's the kid's name, Leon?"

"It's Nathan," said Leon.

"Good. Don't forget, guys, the kid's name is Nathan." Frank put down his guitar and picked up his banjo. "Ready, guys? Let's go…one, two, three…"

Frank began "Tom Dooley" with the banjo solo introduction. Then Ernie and Leon joined in on guitar. So far they sounded great. Then they began to sing. My ears threatened to sue or shut down permanently. The last time I heard a sound like that, my sister was getting her booster shots. They gave new meaning to the word "rehearse." In their case it meant that the hearse would be back to get them later. I was really trying hard to keep an expressionless face. I hoped that the kids at the party weren't going to have their cake and ice cream before ELF went on. If so the parents were going to have a huge clean-up job ahead of them. This group didn't need four songs. As bad as they sounded, all they had to do would be to start any song and people would gladly pay them fifteen dollars to leave early. I was glad I wasn't going to the party.

All of a sudden they stopped and started cracking up with laughter. They were all looking at me. Did my true feelings show? Now I started to worry. "Joey," said Leon through his laughter, "you were great. It must have been hard to keep a straight face. We don't really sound that bad. We just wanted to see how you would react if we sounded really awful. You were very polite. You conceal pain well." So the joke was on me. It was a pretty good joke. I finally relaxed and laughed with them.

They started their show over again. This time they did sound pretty good. They weren't great, but you could listen to them without recalling the Sunday school definition for hell. The skit, four songs, and "Happy Birthday" along with a little goofing around lasted exactly twenty-seven minutes. They decided they had better learn "Scarlet Ribbons" for insurance and in another hour they had it down pretty well. I was impressed especially with Frank. He played banjo on four songs and guitar on "Happy Birthday" and "Scarlet Ribbons." After they had the show ready to their satisfaction, there was even a little time for them to teach me a few guitar chords. Frank let me use his guitar. He said it was easier to mush the strings down when they were nylon. I felt a sense of accomplishment that I would be going home knowing how to play the C-chord and the G-chord on the guitar.

CHAPTER 17

Three-legged Walking

Beginning at suppertime, Frieda initiated a strategy of guerilla warfare. While pouring milk in my glass, she intentionally dripped milk across my plate and into my lap. When nobody was looking, she would stick her tongue out at me. When she did, I would just raise my hand with thumb and little finger extended in opposite directions and the other fingers curled inward so that the thumb touched my ear and the little finger was in front of my mouth. I guess this suggested a telephone to her and she turned a deep red. This seemed to provoke her even more. The next time she went by me she gave me a hard elbow in the back. This happened several more times as it was her turn to replenish milk, coffee, bread, and so on. She had a knack for knowing when nobody was looking.

I needed a defense plan. I noticed that if I sat forward in my chair, it had a tendency to tip forward raising the back several inches. The next time she went behind my chair, I tipped forward slightly at just the right moment. Her elbow crashed against the chair's back and she let out a howl. "Oh! I'm sorry!" I said with my most sincere voice. "You must have slipped. Are you hurt?" It even sounded like I cared. I just love both physics and geometry.

"I'm okay!" she yelped and ran into the kitchen. Cindy, who had seen what Frieda was doing, tried to hold back a smirk. Uncle Fred said "Nice counter-move, Joey" and winked at Cindy who lost it and burst out laughing. I didn't know that he was at all aware of what was going on. I guess he didn't miss much. Aunt Leona looked quizzically at Uncle Fred who said to her, "I'll explain it to you later." She gave a clueless smile and went back to eating. Leon simply kept on eating and seemed not to notice that anything had happened. Leon was clearly not a multi-task kind of person.

By the time Frieda returned from the kitchen, everyone had settled back to eating supper. Frieda carried a basket of bread in one hand and dropped an ice cube down my back with the other. I tried to act like nothing had happened. Uncle Fred would probably deal with it later. It appeared to be a standoff with her getting in the greater number of shots and me inflicting the most damage.

After supper, Uncle Fred and Leon went down to the recreation room in the basement to get things ready for the heavyweight title fight later that night. I offered to help. They said they could handle it but asked if I would go with Cindy to the store to get some pop. As we walked to Walgreen's, Cindy offered sympathy over Frieda's newest assault tactics. "She's really getting dirty now," said Cindy. "I think she's taking a correspondence course in guerilla warfare from Fidel Castro. I'm sure glad that Dad noticed what was going on. You have to watch out for him. He sees more than you think he does. I have to keep remembering that."

"I was surprised to see that he had noticed. I thought she could slip anything past him that she wanted. I wonder if she realizes that she can't. And I think you have it backward. I think Castro is taking classes from Frieda."

"Well, at least you scored the most effective blow of the battle," said Cindy with a smile. "I'll bet her elbow stings for a week."

"Yeah. Well, she's too young and inexperienced to come out ahead in this game," I said. "It sure looks like she'll keep me on my toes though. I think I'll play defense for a while."

We continued discussing possible strategies to use on Frieda until we reached Walgreen's. After making our purchase, we left the store each carrying a six-bottle carton of pop. For a while we just walked quietly. Cindy was the first to speak. "Do you think Glenn and Frieda will listen in the next time you talk to Erica?"

"I doubt it," I said, "although I'm ready if they do. In fact, I'm going to call her as soon as we get back to the house. We have to work out some of the details for Thursday. She's babysitting tonight away from home so we won't have to worry about Glenn listening in. You know, I was just thinking, that will be the last time I see her on this trip. I wonder when I'll see her again."

For a moment, Cindy's expression became pensive, almost as though she knew something that I didn't. Before I could ask what was wrong, she smiled and changed the subject. "Did you ever try a three-legged walk without having your leg tied to the other person's?" she asked. "Here, let's try it."

We switched the pop cartons to our outside hands and put our arms around each other's waist. Then we walked so that our inside legs appeared to be tied together. It was fun. It was goofy. Cindy smelled nice. By the time we arrived home we had tried several variations of walking together—in-step, out-of-step, and syncopated step. We must have looked like the Marx Brothers. As we entered the kitchen, I reluctantly took my hand from Cindy's waist and helped her load the pop into the refrigerator. When we were finished, I went to the den to call Erica.

CHAPTER 18

Second Phone Call to Erica

I dialed the number Erica had given me. "Hello, Mason's residence," she answered.

"Hi, Erica. It's me, Joey," I said.

"Hi, Joey. I'm glad you called now. The two kids I'm babysitting are watching a boring TV show that their mother says they watch every week. I can still keep an eye on them while I talk to you," said Erica.

"Good," I said. "Say, did Glenn say anything about what we did to him and Frieda last night?"

"Oh no, he wouldn't dare!" she exclaimed with glee. "But I could tell that it worked. I was telling my parents about your call at breakfast. All of a sudden I said to Glenn, 'In fact, Glenn, Joey has a cousin named Frieda. You know Frieda, don't you?' He really turned red. I think he was afraid that I would ask him to take Frieda to the party with us. He was really nervous."

"That's great!" I said. "Frieda reacted the same way when I made a fake phone with my hand and put it to my ear. Cindy is going to try to get them together a few times just to watch them squirm. I wish I could see that." Then, changing the subject, I asked, "How was your day today?"

"Actually I had a pretty nice day. I went shopping for some clothes with my mom this morning and I played tennis with three of my girlfriends this afternoon. And now I'm talking to you. How about you? How was your day?" Erica asked.

"I guess I'd have to call this day strange. Up to now, that is. Do you know a guy named Mad Dog Norkus?" I asked.

"Everyone knows Mad Dog. So you met him today. That must have been an experience. Tell me about it," she said enthusiastically.

I told her about the escapade with Mr. Shaker and the bulldog. Then I told her about the basketball game, making sure that she knew that I was the hero of the game (at least in my own mind). Of course I did this with great modesty.

"So you had a short game that only went to two hundred points. How long did the game take?" she asked.

"It only lasted two hours," I said. "But I suppose it would have taken longer if we had taken a half-time break. Besides, we had to get home in time for lunch. And Leon had a rehearsal with his folk group this afternoon. That was an experience too."

"I'll bet it was. By the way, I was talking to Phyllis just before I came over here to babysit and she asked if we would be going to see Leon's group at their first paying job. When did that come up?" she asked.

"I'm not sure," I replied. "I found out about it this morning. It's no problem though. Leon's expecting me to go with you to the pool party. Anyway, I heard their act today. They are pretty good, although there were times when I wasn't sure they would be. They didn't even have a name until this afternoon. They agreed on ELF. That was my suggestion. You should have heard some of the other suggestions, especially Ernie's. He's weird."

"Well, it's different. What does elf mean?" she asked.

"The letters E-L-F stand for Ernie, Leon, and Frank," I explained.

"I like it," she said. "How do they sound as a group? Are they like any of the better known groups?"

"Not really," I said. "I mean that they don't really sound like anybody else. They've done something to give themselves a unique sound. The problem is they only know five songs, six if you count 'Happy Birthday.' They learned a new one today. Maybe by the end of the summer they will know enough songs to get jobs in the coffee houses. And Frank is pretty good instrumentally. He is very good on the five-string banjo and he plays a strong melody on guitar rather than just strumming chords."

"Phyllis and I are supposed to go hear them rehearse next week," said Erica. "Now I'm kind of looking forward to it.

"It looks like I'll have to drive Thursday. My parents already said I could. In fact, they said that it would be okay if you drove the car once I picked you up."

"That's fine. I'll be happy to drive if you want me to, but really, I don't care who drives. I'll just be happy to be with you. What time do you want me to be ready?" I asked.

"Oh, darn. I forgot what time the party starts," she replied. "I'll have to check and tell you tomorrow night. Oh my, I just realized that we could have taken care of all this tomorrow night. I'm glad that didn't occur to you. Otherwise, we wouldn't be talking tonight. I enjoy talking to you, Joey."

"Oh, it occurred to me, but I would have been stupid to mention it. I enjoy talking to you too, Erica." We were clearly on the same wave length. I was starting to get the same feeling I had after our date Saturday night. I guess I wouldn't hear Leon snore tonight either. "I'll see you tomorrow at seven-thirty. Bye now."

"Bye, Joey," she said sweetly.

I put the phone down gently and just sat there not wanting to give up the feeling that I was experiencing. All of a sudden there were several loud thuds on the door. "Joey! They're waiting for you downstairs. The fight is going to start pretty soon." That broke the mood. It was Frieda, snotty as ever. I'll bet she was listening outside the door the whole time.

CHAPTER 19

The Fight

The party was well in progress by the time I got downstairs to the recreation room. I heard Mad Dog even before I reached the stairs. When I got to the basement I saw Marc, Ken, Ernie, and Frank were also there. The seven of us had the basement to ourselves. Frieda and Cindy were upstairs watching TV with Aunt Leona and Uncle Fred. There was a radio in the middle of a large coffee table with chairs and cushions all around. On the floor at either end of the coffee table were two large baskets full of buttered popcorn. By the door was a metal tub full of ice and pop. The guys were talking but would periodically stop and listen to the radio to see if the fight was about to start. Leon looked up as I reached the bottom of the stairs. "Well, lover boy, you finally got off the phone," he said. It felt to me like I blushed a little. Several other guys greeted me with the more standard "Hi, Joey!"

"Hey, Joey. I hear you're going out with Erica Andersen," said Mad Dog enviously. "She's a real chick. I asked her out once but she said she had to take her parakeet to the vet." I couldn't believe he fell for that one. The other guys started hooting and howling and throwing kernels of popcorn at Mad Dog. He caught as many as he could and ate them.

"Did you hear the first fight between Patterson and Johansson, Joey?" asked Marc.

"I sure did," I responded. "I can still remember Howard Cosell interviewing Floyd Patterson after he lost the fight. Remember when he asked, 'Well, Floyd, whatta ya gonna do now?'" I gave my best Howard Cosell mimic. "And Floyd just said, 'Howard, I just don't know.' I mean, here's a guy who's probably still dizzy from having lost the heavyweight championship to Ingemar Johansson by a knock-out, and here comes a commentator asking a dumb, insensitive question like that."

"Yeah. It's a good thing Floyd is such a classy guy," added Ken. "Someday Cosell is going to ask a question like that to the wrong guy, then look out."

"Hey, I think Floyd should have given him his best punch and then said, 'Well, Howard, I'm going to knock out at least one white guy tonight," injected Mad Dog. Everyone laughed at that, even though we could not picture Floyd Patterson standing over a comatose Howard Cosell. None of us had any trouble picturing Cosell on his back with his microphone pointed heavenward.

"Quiet down, guys," Said Frank. "The fight's getting ready to start."

"Yeah! Quiet everyone," said Leon.

"Hey, we have to do something to keep Mad Dog quiet," said Marc. "I know, let's do what we did at the last fight. Mad Dog, you be Patterson. Who's going to be Johansson?"

"I'll do it!" said Ernie. "Okay, Floyd baby, get ready. I'm gonna knock you out again."

It was perfect casting. Patterson was not a talker. He was a very quiet fighter. He let his fists do the talking. Mad Dog would have to be a great actor to carry that off.

The commentary began as the bell sounded the start of the first round. Mad Dog danced around imitating the peek-a-boo style of Floyd Patterson. Ernie continuously stalked his opponent. They were actually pretty good. Of course we had all seen the newsreel footage of the first fight. They even seemed to be following the blow-by-blow description of the fight pretty well. During each round the rest of us, having picked sides, cheered, ate popcorn, and drank pop. At the end of each round, we would get up, go to the corner of our favored fighter, give them a swig of pop, wipe their forehead with a dirty old rag, and ignore the commercial. During the second round those of us who were cheering for Patterson got quite a scare. Johansson unloaded his famous "toonder and lightning" punch, a right high on the head of Patterson. Patterson retreated and, somehow, survived. Mad Dog really put on an act. He was stumbling around, staggering, doubled over, hanging onto the ropes, hanging onto Ernie, and finally he started tickling Ernie. The tickling wasn't in the commentary.

Finally, in the fifth round, Patterson threw a few quick punches and Ingemar Johansson was down for the count. Patterson had done it. He was the first heavyweight to regain the title. We all cheered, even Ernie after he got up off the floor. Leon shouted, "Does anyone want to listen and see if Cosell asks Ingemar what he's going to do now?" Nobody did. He turned off the radio and we finished up the evening eating popcorn, drinking pop, and playing euchre and checkers.

Since there were seven of us, I invited Cindy to come down and join us so we would have an even number. Everybody except Leon thought that was a good idea so Leon cut his loses and just kept quiet about it.

CHAPTER 20

The Queen of Chinese Checkers

We awoke Tuesday to dark skies and the sound of thunder and rain rapping sharply against the window pane. It was certain that our plans for the renewal of hoop ball hostilities would have to be postponed. Fortunately our evening plans involved indoor activities. Leon sat up, threw his legs over the side of the bed, stretched, yawned, and shook his head vigorously. Then he took a look out the window, saw the rain, rolled back into bed, and went back to sleep for another hour. I wondered if he would repeat the ritual when he woke up again.

By this time I was wide awake. I decided to go shave (for the third time since school let out two weeks ago) and then read the morning paper. I had mixed feelings about shaving. I liked being mature enough to need to shave; I disliked the process of shaving. I hoped that I would live long enough to either see beards come back into fashion or to have access to a space-age invention that would give you a clean, close, comfortable shave at the touch of a button. My dad says he's waiting for the same thing and he'll be irreconcilably peeved if one or the other does not put in an appearance soon.

I went downstairs to the family room and looked for the morning paper. Uncle Fred had already gone to work, Aunt Leona was in the basement sorting laundry for Frieda to finish, and Frieda and Cindy were playing Chinese checkers in front of the dormant fire place. I greeted Cindy and Frieda as I entered the room. When I sat down and picked up the paper, Cindy got up and went out to the kitchen. She returned with a glass of orange juice and a plate holding the plumpest glazed donut I had ever seen. "Here, Joey," she said, smiling. "We already had breakfast but I saved you a donut."

"Thanks, Cindy," I said. "That was really thoughtful." Her smile broadened. Then she turned and resumed her game with Frieda. I took a bite of the donut. It was every bit as good as it looked. I was really getting spoiled. I couldn't imagine my sister treating me this way. I picked up the sports section and read all of the articles about the Patterson-Johansson fight of the night before. There were articles about the fight, interviews with both fighters from before and after the fight and even an article about all the previous heavyweights who had lost the title and tried to regain it. Patterson was the first to succeed in recapturing the heavyweight crown. Already there was talk of another rematch and predictions of its outcome. I finished the orange juice, the donut, and the sports section all at about the same time. After reading the comics, I picked up the business section and tried to look as though I understood it. I wasn't really sure why I wanted to impress Cindy but I did. After about three minutes of bluffing, I put the paper down and walked over to the fireplace to watch Cindy and Frieda. They were just finishing a game. It looked like Frieda had won. Actually, it sounded like Frieda had won. "Beat you again!" boasted Frieda. "Nobody beats Frieda. I'm the queen of Chinese checkers. Don't feel too bad. You were beaten by the best."

"And you're so humble," I said. "What a remarkable combination."

Cindy laughed. "Why don't you play, Joey?" Cindy offered. "We can play three-way."

"I think I will," I said, taking up the offer. "This looks interesting, but you'll have to show me how to play." Of course I knew how to play but I wanted to catch Frieda off-guard. I could work with Cindy and together we could defeat her. I just wanted Frieda to think that I was lucky or a real genius to pick up the game so fast. We played a practice game in which Cindy explained the rules and suggested some strategies. I blundered along and occasionally asked a mildly stupid question. Frieda would roll her eyes at me as Cindy patiently explained.

As we were about to begin a serious game, Frieda could no longer keep quiet. "This is pathetic," she said disdainfully. "I'll mop you both up in no time flat. It hardly seems worth my effort, but it's raining and there's nothing else to do." She sighed and made her first move. Sighs of disdain soon became sighs of disbelief and then sighs of despair. Cindy and I clobbered her and then continued on the rest of the game, which I eventually won.

"Gosh!" I said. "It must be beginner's luck. This is a strange game. I really didn't know what I was doing and I won. I can't believe it." I winked at Cindy who, by now, had guessed the truth.

"You did play pretty well, Joey," said Cindy. "Let's play again. I'm sure Frieda wants another chance at you, right, Frieda?"

"I'll play again," she said bitterly. "No hick town clown can beat me and get away with it. Move, Joey." She said the last two words through her nose with such vehemence that I hoped for permanent damage to her sinuses. And move I did. Again, Cindy and I combined forces to put her out of the game early. This time, after destroying Frieda, I played terribly (on purpose) and Cindy crushed me.

Frieda stormed out and started up the stairs. Cindy called after her. "Don't forget, Mom has some laundry downstairs for you to do." Frieda's storming now took on a more audible tone.

This was followed by Aunt Leona's call from the kitchen as she came up from the basement. "Frieda, I've finished sorting the laundry. You need to go down to the basement and put a load in the washing machine. There are only three loads today and just one has shirts in it that will need to be ironed. Move along now, dear."

Frieda's fuming became a long, mournful moan as she turned on the stairs and tramped down to the basement. As soon as she was out of the room, Cindy and I started laughing, quietly, so as not to alert Aunt Leona. At first we were sitting back-to-back with our heads bent forward in glee. Then Cindy turned and put her arms around my neck from behind, resting her chin on my shoulder. I was about to offer her a fifteen-minute time limit to desist from this activity when she said, "I think you fooled her, Joey. She just didn't want to believe you were smart enough to beat her twice, and the way you played the last half of the last game convinced her you weren't. It was nice of you to let me win. After the way she had clobbered me earlier, I was starting to get depressed."

"Come on, cousin," I said, "I didn't exactly let you win. You were playing pretty well. When I could see you would probably win anyway, I decided to look especially bad for Frieda's sake. Besides, you smell too nice to beat at Chinese checkers."

She released her hold around my neck, got up, picked up my plate and juice glass, and took them out to the kitchen. She was blushing a little as she left the family room.

Before I got too caught up in my thoughts Leon came downstairs and sat down to read the paper. "Looks like our basketball game has been rained out," he said without looking up from the sports section. "Do you play chess?"

"Yeah," I answered. "Why?"

"Are you any good?" he asked, ignoring my question.

"I guess I'm good enough," I responded. "I beat our pastor at the altar boy picnic this spring, and my dad says the pastor is a really good chess player. Why?"

"Have you ever played with a clock?" he continued, again ignoring my question.

"I didn't know clocks could play chess," I said impatiently. "*Why* are you asking me this?"

"Oh, I just thought we might kill some time this afternoon playing speed chess. Ken, Marc, and Skip all play and we have to invite RG3 because he is president of the chess club at school and has the chess clocks. The only problem is that he always wins. I was hoping you might be good enough to give him a run for his money."

"And who is RG3, pray tell?" I asked.

"RG3 is Richard Gilbert Thornton the Third. He prefers to be called RG, which he says stands for Real Genius. We compromised on RG3 which, unbeknownst to him, means Richard Gilbert, Real Genius? Really Goofy! He always wears a white shirt, tie, and a sports coat, has his hair slicked back perfectly combed, and wears black horn-rimmed glasses that are too small for his face. At school he also carries a slide rule in a kind of holster strapped to his belt. Some day they will probably have a name for people like this." Leon seemed to really enjoy describing RG3.

"Okay. So now I have a vague idea who RG3 is," I continued. "Now what is this about chess clocks?"

"A chess clock is really a box that contains two clocks," explained Leon. By now he had put down the paper. "Above each clock is a button. When you push down the button, it stops the clock below it and starts the other clock, your opponent's clock. After a pre-set time has elapsed, a flag inside the clock falls and that person loses if they haven't made a specified number of moves or won the game. This is called a time forfeit. For normal games, you have two hours to make forty moves. In speed chess each clock is set for five minutes for a complete game to be played. If your flag falls, you lose. It's not hard to learn to use a clock. What do you think, should I call the guys?"

"I've never played with a clock before," I said, "but it sounds like fun. Let's give it a try."

CHAPTER 21

The Speed Chess Tournament

Marc, Ken, Skip and RG3 arrived shortly after lunch and we all went down to the basement. RG3 looked exactly as Leon described him. I didn't think any kid would wear a sport coat and tie on purpose unless he were forced. RG3 blew that theory to pieces. Skip and Ken each gave me a couple of practice games so I could get used to the clock and the other rules of speed chess. The way they played, a game of speed chess never lasted the full ten minutes. We then set up a round robin tournament so that we played each person twice, once with white and once with black pieces. Leon made sure that I would play RG3 in the last round. In the first round I played Marc and lost the first game playing the black pieces. After that I won seven straight games. For the last round, I drew the white pieces for the first game against RG3. After my third move he started commenting. "Aha!" he exclaimed. "The Giuoco Piano. I must play to avoid the Fried Liver." With that he made his move.

All of a sudden I noticed that we were the only ones playing. The others had stopped and were watching our game. I guess it didn't matter much. RG3 had won all of his games so far and had a score of 8-0. I had lost only one game and had a score of 7-1. One of us would be the champion. Of course I had no idea what he was talking about so I decided to make it look like I was faking ignorance. "I had no idea that you were interested in the piano," I answered. "I do, however, wish you would not discuss your menu for supper. I see you've chosen the BLT variation. I thought you might." In making my next move I tried to convince him with body language that he was doomed.

His eyes widened and his jaw dropped. "I've never seen that variation before," he exclaimed cautiously. His next move was a little tentative.

The next ten or fifteen moves went quickly and I began to see that I had a strong attack. I pushed my rook all the way down to his end of the board, not realizing that I had just given checkmate. RG3 stopped the clock, reached over, and we shook hands. Game one was mine and we were tied for the Speed Chess Championship of the Known Universe (pre-Star Trek). He hurried off to the bathroom, probably hoping to reassure himself he could win the deciding game. The other guys were going nuts. Skip said, "I've never seen him lose before."

"This is the first time I've ever seen him look so worried," exclaimed Ken.

"Don't let him bluff you with all those names he tosses out for the moves. He's about the only one I know who had read a book on chess and I think he is just trying to impress you," warned Leon.

Marc also added some advice. "If it looks like he's giving away a piece for nothing, call it a gambit. Call everything else a variation and give it a Russian- or German-sounding name. He'll think you've read something he hasn't and go to pieces."

"I think we may see a new champion today," said Skip with obvious glee.

RG3 returned and we began the final, decisive game. It looked like he was offering me a free pawn. "Aha!" I said. "The Stuermer Gambit." I responded quickly by moving out my knight and ignoring the offered pawn.

"Now I know you're bluffing," he exclaimed, making his move. "That was the Evan's Gambit."

"Sure. That's its common name," I said with a superior tone. "But this is a special variation played by the Prussian grandmaster Cedric Stuermer against the Archduke of Brittany in 1857. Stuermer's win from this point is practically forced." I made my next move with renewed confidence. If I could pull this off, I could probably make a good living in sales.

He hesitated, reached for a piece, drew his hand back, and reached again. He could not make up his mind. He was obviously buying what I was selling. He hesitated again and then very gingerly made his move.

"I can't believe it!" I exclaimed. After all, in for a penny, in for a pound. "You've made the Kavinowski Blunder."

He looked at the board, then at me, then back at the board. I tried to maintain the expression of disbelief as I also looked at the board. Then I saw it. If he continued to play and play correctly, he would checkmate me in three moves. His hand moved slowly toward the bishop, which would set up the kill. Then he drew his hand back, reached for his king, set the king on its side, and stopped the clock. He had not seen the move. He was conceding the game. I had not uttered an honest statement since the game began. I had won the match and the championship on a bluff. Of course he started it. He was trying to do the same thing. There was one difference between us: commitment.

I was being congratulated from all sides. Even RG3 seemed to be taking it pretty well. "Hey, why don't you two guys play a serious game? How about it, RG3?" suggested Leon.

"Okay," said RG3. "But we play by the rules. Touch move and no talking during the match. You guys can't help either one of us."

CHAPTER 22

RG3 and the Death Match

We sat down and drew for color. I got the white pieces. Leon, aware that I didn't know how to write down the moves using chess notation, suggested that the six guys who were not playing would write down the moves for both of us so that we would be free to contemplate our moves and press the button on the clock with the same hand we used to move a piece. RG3 quickly agreed to this since the clock is always set on black's right (white's left) and we were both left-handed. This gave him two disadvantages right from the start. Not having to record the game as he played seemed to ease his mind a bit.

We set up the board, adjusted the clock for two hours each (to make forty moves), and began. As we started the game I felt pretty good. I was unconcerned about the outcome. After all, I had bluffed my way through the speed tournament. What difference could one more game make? The first three moves went pretty quickly. After a minute or two of thought, I played my fourth move. At this point RG3 looked carefully at the board, sat back, and closed his eyes for two solid minutes. I was afraid that he was going to sleep. Suddenly he opened his eyes widely, sat forward, and stared again at the board. His eyes darted from piece to piece. It was beginning to look like he actually knew what was going on. Then, with great deliberateness, he castled.

The guys began to look back and forth at one another. Nobody said anything but it was clear that everyone was involved with the game. They took their chess seriously, even if they didn't know much about the game. They also seemed to expect me to beat an opponent who had probably forgotten more about chess than I ever knew. All of a sudden I began to feel nervous. I felt a knot in my stomach, my hands started to sweat, and I was getting a headache. The next several moves were made more slowly. Both of us were being very cautious. He certainly did not seem to be attacking me, but he did seem to be building up material on the queen's side of the board. I was not yet ready to attack either. I could tell that RG3 was nervous too because he had loosened his tie and removed his jacket.

I had figured the game might last an hour or so. Before I realized it, we had played more than two-and-a-half hours and had arrived at what I thought was a very complicated position. I had just made a move and looked up to see that Cindy had joined the group to watch the game. The sense of pressure increased. I now felt that I had to win.

At about the three-hour mark, Frieda brought down lemonade for everyone. Everyone, that is, except RG3 and me. She stood by the board, waited until it was my move, and then announced loudly, "Sorry, guys, I couldn't carry all the lemonade in one trip. I'll go up now and get yours. Be right back." And she trotted off.

A few moments later she returned with a tray holding two glasses of lemonade. At least I hoped it was lemonade. I made my move just as she set the glass down next to RG3. She then walked around the table and held the tray toward me. Realizing that I was extremely thirsty, I reached for the glass. Just as I was about to lift it, I knew why she had not set the glass down beside me. She had brushed some kind of oil all over the outside of the glass. I released the glass and left it on the tray. I said quietly, "Nice try, Frieda, but I'll pass." She pouted, turned, and walked up the basement steps with Cindy close behind.

Having narrowly avoided another embarrassment at Frieda's hands, I tried to return my thoughts to the game. I still had an internal thirst that would not go away. Cindy returned a moment later and set a glass of lemonade beside me and whispered, "This one's safe. I poured it myself."

"Thank you," I whispered back and took several swallows.

These distractions were eroding my concentration. I had to get back in the game. I surveyed the board and saw that we were even in material and neither of us threatened a strong attack. Maybe if I could trade off most of the remaining pieces, I might get at least a draw. I decided to try. It was getting late and Leon and I had dates for that night. I led off with the first of many exchanges. As the trades continued, prospects for a draw seemed to increase. RG3 was now biting his nails. I have always found this a disgusting habit, which I confine to the privacy of my room. Being a curious person, I watched him closely to see what happened to the fingernail after he had chewed it off. He must have either parked them in his cheek or swallowed them because I never once saw a nail leave his mouth. Suddenly I realized I was being distracted again. Now being distracted by Cindy was one thing, but being distracted by a nail-biter was ridiculous.

RG3 was down to having only his king while I had a king and a pawn. On top of that, my king was in front of my pawn. I knew I should be able to win but I wasn't exactly sure how to go about it. I must have looked confident, however, because at this point, RG3 sighed, stood up, tipped over his king, and extended his hand. He was resigning. The guys huddled around both of us and congratulated us on the good game. It had lasted just under four hours. I had never played a game before that lasted more than one hour. I was drained. The knot in my stomach was loosening but I still had a slight headache. It had been the toughest game I'd ever been in and I was glad it was over.

"Hey, Joey." It was RG3. "When are you going to be back in Chicago?"

"I don't know, RG," I replied. "Why do you ask?"

He laughed. "I think I want to plan to be out of town. You're a tough opponent. Good game."

"Thanks. You're pretty tough yourself. I don't think I'll come looking for you." I meant it too.

"Tell me, Joey," he said, "was Cedric Stuermer bluff or real?"

I smiled, then turned, and walked up the basement steps. Who knows. I might end up playing chess with him again. I hoped I would have enough energy for bowling tonight.

CHAPTER 23

"Brains"

After supper, two aspirin, and a shower, I felt like a new person. I was a little nervous about tonight, this time because I still didn't know Erica real well and I was unsure of myself. I didn't want to mess things up. We hadn't known each other long enough to become comfortable in the knowledge of what the other liked or disliked. I had hoped that, like Saturday night, the feelings of uneasiness would evaporate early in the evening.

Leon had not been preoccupied with tonight. He was still thinking about the chess matches this afternoon. "Gee, Joey," he said, "I didn't know you were so good at chess. Do you have a chess club in your high school?"

"No, we don't," I responded. "But there are four other guys and one girl in our school who like to play and we play during lunch and sometimes after school."

"You must have read a lot about the game," he continued. "RG never heard of Cedric Stuermer and he reads everything. He's always got a chess book that he's working on and he has subscriptions to two chess magazines. I can't believe you stumped him."

"Please don't tell anyone, Leon," I said confidentially, "but I never heard of Cedric Stuermer either."

"You mean that whole thing was a bluff?" he said with great surprise.

"It sure was," I replied with a laugh. "In fact, if he had looked carefully at that last move, he would have seen that he could have checkmated me in three moves. I guess he was thinking too much about Cedric Stuermer and not enough about the position."

"That's incredible!" he said with amazement. "He'd go nuts if he ever found out. I'm sure not going to be the one to tell him. What made you think of trying a bluff?"

"Well, we have a guy in our class who is quite a bit like RG. He's smart and he uses his intelligence like a weapon. He tries to overpower everyone with it. His name is Brian but we call him "Brains." Choose your own inflections. Anyway, one day we got a new student in class whose father had been transferred to Benton Harbor from Alpena. I think he was a Kroger manager. Apparently this kid was pretty smart too. His name was Vince. One day we were all sitting around the lunch table talking about the insect collection we had to do for biology class. We were each giving hints as to where to find various kinds of insects. Well, "Brains" started to give us a scholarly dissertation about the art of locating and classifying insects. I don't know why he had bothered to look all that stuff up because we found out later that he had bought his insect collection from a scientific supply house and replaced all the professionally printed identification tags with his own hand-printed tags. In fact his mother had even done the printing. About the only thing he did was to bring it to school.

Anyway, when "Brains" had finished his unsolicited presentation, Vince calmly pointed out that he was correct as far as he went, but that he had failed to comment on three obscure species of insects indigenous to the sand dunes in our area. Vince then went into detail about the habits of these insects and exactly how to find and catch them.

"A couple of weeks later," I continued, "we found out that Vince had been bluffing. Vince doesn't usually show off his intelligence except on tests. "Brains" must have spent hours slogging through the sand dunes looking for the insects figuring this would really impress the teacher if he could add them to his store-bought collection. Then he spent hours in the library trying to verify Vince's facts. Finally, he accused Vince of fraud. Of course, Vince didn't deny it. He just suggested that maybe someone should try to verify everything that "Brains" had told us. The subject got changed in a hurry.

Later I asked Vince about his deception. He told me that there were two things to remember about a person like "Brains." First, they lack confidence. Second, give them enough time and they will tell you everything they know and then make up a lot more to go with it. Then all you have to do is reveal some "new information" that challenges the shakiest information that they dispensed. Their own lack of confidence will prevent them from challenging anything they have not specifically read on the subject. I guess Vince was right. It worked against RG, didn't it?"

"It sure did," agreed Leon. "But, you know, it only seems to work for an outsider. The brains of this world usually have the people who are around them a lot figured out. It's the newcomer who fools them."

"I hadn't thought of that," I said. Suddenly I noticed the clock on the dresser. "Say, Leon, we better get going or we'll be late."

"Gosh, you're right. Let's hustle." We each grabbed a light jacket. Though the rain had stopped just before supper, it was still overcast and there was a damp chill in the air. Downstairs we said a hurried good-bye to Aunt Leona and Uncle Fred, ran out to the car, and were on our way.

CHAPTER 24

The Bowling Date

We picked up Phyllis first. I waited in the car while Leon went up to the door. Phyllis was ready and met him at the door. "Hi, Joey," she said cheerfully as she entered the car.

"Hi, Phyllis," I said. "How do you like this weather?" I was always clever at initiating conversations.

"Actually, I didn't like it much until now," she answered as Leon got in. "But now I think it's great. It gives us an excuse to cuddle." She slid over to Leon and melted into his side.

It was a short ride over to Erica's house and nobody said much. Leon pulled into the driveway and I went up to the door to get Erica. She was ready too, but she asked me to come in so her parents could meet me. "It was my idea," she whispered. I took that as a good sign. I tried to smile and appear friendly and completely harmless.

Erica managed the introductions with effortless poise. Sometimes you get the feeling you are being given the visual third degree by parents equipped with radar capable of exposing your innermost thoughts and desires. That was not the case here. Her parents seemed very trusting and extremely friendly. Without saying it, they conveyed the message that they were very glad to meet me because their daughter liked me. When the obligatory small talk was completed, we made our way to the door and out toward the car. "Don't worry about being late. Just drive carefully," Mr. Andersen called out after us.

"Thanks, Dad," said Erica. "We'll be careful. See you later."

Feeling that I understood the procedure, I opened the door for Erica and then followed her into the car. Leon, having learned from a master, initiated the conversation. "How ya doin', Erica?" he said. "How do you like this weather?"

"I didn't think much of it this afternoon, but I'm beginning to see the good points," she said as she snuggled up close to me. I lifted my arm and put it around her as she rested her head on my shoulder. Her hair was softly curled and had the fresh smell of a forest after a cool summer rain. Here I was hopelessly stuck in *now*, again. I was about to suggest that we find a bowling alley in Dubuque.

Leon pulled out of the driveway and we were on our way. At this point, Leon felt compelled to relate to the girls the events of this afternoon. He embellished the story to the point of embarrassment (even more than I would have). Of course, he had to tell them about the big bluff. That really got them to giggling. His story was far better than my memory of what had happened. Judging from the smiles and admiring glances from Erica, Leon was doing a fine job of promoting the value of Joey Winters's stock. I was glad to own 100 percent interest in the company.

We arrived at a bowling alley considerably east of Dubuque at about the same time as Leon started to run out of ways to exaggerate my greatness this afternoon. It was time to literally and figuratively get my feet back on the ground. Think about it. What could be more enjoyable than having someone expound on your prowess to a beautiful girl snuggled up close beside you? Unfortunately everything that goes up must come down. The cause of my ego's descent tonight would probably be my bowling. I was the only person I knew who could consistently follow a strike with two gutter balls. At least tonight I was ready with an excuse that should work to my benefit. I would claim that I could not keep my mind on the game because of the distracting beauty of my date. And I wouldn't be lying either. When I looked at Erica, it was impossible for me to think of anything else.

We were assigned an alley, rented shoes, and went off to hunt down a ball that was comfortable. We decided that we would play a couples challenge: Phyllis and Leon against Erica and me. I hoped that Erica was a good bowler because I was probably going to need her help. Phyllis started off followed by Erica, then Leon and then me. In the first frame Phyllis and Erica each got a spare and Leon and I each rolled a strike. I knew that in my case it couldn't last. I was right. Phyllis got nine pins in the next frame, Erica rolled a split and settled for nine pins, Leon got a spare, and I had a grand total of three pins. At this point, I decided to try to be relaxed and act as though the game was just for fun anyway. The first game ended with Phyllis and Leon fifteen pins ahead of Erica and me. Phyllis had rolled a 113 and Leon had a 167. Erica was the big surprise. She was an excellent bowler. She had a 163, just four pins behind Leon. My score was an embarrassing 102.

Between the first and second game Leon and I got soft drinks for the girls and ourselves. After the drinks were half finished, we resumed bowling. The results were about the same as the first game. We were now 34 pins behind primarily due to my 97. I tried hard to act like I was having fun anyway, but I did feel disconcerted by my poor bowling.

I suspect that Erica may have sensed my distress. Between games as we were sitting and finishing our soft drinks, she took my hand and whispered in my ear, "I'm having a great time tonight, and it's only because I'm with you, Joey." Then she gave me a quick kiss on the cheek. I knew I could forget the bowling score of that evening, but I would remember that moment with Erica forever.

We were just about to begin our third game when an announcement came over the loudspeaker. "Our summer Tuesday night bowling league will begin play at ten o'clock. We ask all bowlers to finish their games by that time. Thank you for your patronage."

We had about thirty-five minutes to complete our third game. We agreed that we would probably have time. Without thinking I said, "I guess we'll just have to roll strikes so we don't delay the league." Then it occurred to me that I was the one who had not rolled his share of strikes.

The last game went pretty much as the first two had gone with only one surprise. Phyllis scored a 121, Leon a 173, and Erica again challenged Leon by rolling a 168. I was the surprise. I started off with six strikes. That was followed by a spare, a nine pin open frame, another spare and three more strikes. I ended up with a 237. I had never done that well before.

Erica and I ended up winning by 77 pins. We all had something to celebrate. Leon had the high three game series, Erica had three games over 150 for the first time in her life, Phyllis had her first three game series without being under a hundred and I had my first 200 game.

CHAPTER 25

Paulo's

Our spirits were high as we left the bowling arcade and drove off in search of the best pizza in town. Erica mentioned that she had heard about a new place close by called Paulo's, which was supposed to have excellent Italian food and was also romantic. I don't think Leon had any better idea than I did about what Erica meant by "romantic" but we both wanted to find out. We had to drive around the block where the restaurant was supposed to be located three times before we found it. We had been looking up for a sign. Paulo's sign was at sidewalk level with an arrow pointing to the basement of a rather large commercial building. We parked the car and found the entrance at the bottom of a flight of stairs located at the corner of the building. There were hanging plants (begonias according to Phyllis) above either side of the entrance. The flowers were bright red and they seemed to be thriving, indicating that they were well taken care of. One pot had "Paulo" hand-painted in green on it and the other pot had "Regina" also hand-painted in green. The door, door frame and the frame around the windows had a carefully applied fresh coat of black paint, which off-set the gray stone of the building. In the window hung a neon "Welcome" sign in the center and a hardware store "OPEN" sign in the corner near the door. Italian music was emanating softly from a speaker above the door. I was already impressed.

We entered to see a very large room that was filled with tables. Some were small and round (seating up to four) and others were long (seating at least eight). All had black wood chairs with red cushion seats. The backs of the chairs were heart-shaped. There was a small bar along one wall and a jukebox against the opposite wall. Next to the bar were a pair of red swinging doors each with a port-hole window. I assumed the kitchen was on the other side. Several of the round tables were occupied by couples and there was a large group of people at a pair of long tables that had been pushed together. They were gathering up their things and getting ready to leave. It looked like a family group celebrating a birthday. It was kind of noisy.

A waiter approached. He was short, thin, and immaculately dressed in a starched white shirt, a black bow tie (not a clip-on), highly polished black shoes, and black tuxedo pants with a gray cummerbund. The bald space on top of his head was surrounded on three sides by short, very black hair, and he had a black, pencil-thin moustache that looked like a check mark below each nostril. I made a mental note not to ask him if his name was Paulo.

"Gooda evening, gentlemen. Buona sera, ladies," he said in what was probably an authentic accent. "Welcome to Paulo's. I'm Paulo." (Honestly, I really wouldn't have asked.) "Woulda you anda the lovely ladies like to be seated ina our dininga room or woulda you prefer the quiet atmosphere ofa our Venice Room?"

"We'd like the Venice Room," I said. It was certainly too noisy in the dining room. Paulo led the way to a single door on the other side of the dining room. As we passed through, it was as though we were entering another country. The room was much smaller than the dining room. There was a fountain in the center of the room with small red and blue spotlights shimmering on it from the ceiling. In each corner of the room was a circular booth with plush velvet seats and high backs. The only light in the room other than the two spotlights aimed at the fountain were large candles with curved glass chimneys in the center of each table. One booth was occupied by a couple and the others were vacant. Paulo seated us in the booth farthest from the other couple, brought us large glasses of ice water and menus.

It was very comfortable in the booth. After the girls had gotten in, Leon and I seated ourselves in the outside seats leaving a respectable distance between ourselves and our respective dates. However, Paulo had left only one menu per couple so it was necessary for us to move closer together so that we could look over the selections. Paulo was no dummy. "I don't know, Phyllis," said Leon in an aside to Phyllis that Erica and I were clearly supposed to overhear. "I don't see fish on the menu. What are we going to do?" With that Phyllis gave Leon an elbow jab in the ribs and started to chuckle.

"Stop it, Leon," she said. "You couldn't carry it off anyway." Then she turned to Erica and said, "Come on, Erica, let's go to the restroom." Then to us, "Excuse us please. You go ahead and order for us. I'm sure you'll pick something we like." They left without waiting for a response.

They were no sooner out of sight than Paulo returned. "May I taka you order?" he asked politely.

"Sure, Paulo," I said. "How about a short course in menu reading. Most of these things I've never seen before. What would you suggest?"

"Aaahhh! We have a dish that isa not even ona the menu. It isa just for a special occasion like this. Your lovely lady friends willa love it." Paulo was really getting into his routine now. "It is a double crust pizza with a richa sauce, three kinds ofa cheese and isa topped with pepperoni, green peppers, mushrooms, sliced green olives, sliced black olives, and bacon. Ita is calleda Calizzo." He pronounced the name Kal-EETS-so.

"Hey, that sounds pretty good, Paulo," agreed Leon. "Let's have one of those. Is it enough for four people?"

"We prepare eacha dish individually so that ita is a meal for one person. We serve it in a porcelain disha so that it will remain hot while it isa eaten. I assure you, it isa very special," answered Paulo.

"It sounds excellent, Paulo," said Leon. "We will each have one. What do you have to drink?"

"We have the usual choices ofa soft drinks, milk, coffee, or tea. But fora you, may I suggest a sparkling and slightly dry, non-alcoholic grape juice. It isa very special. It adds to the ambiance, and it keeps me out of trouble witha the local police. It isa served in chilled champagne glasses. And," he added with a wink, "two bottles are cheaper than four soft drinks." He smiled and awaited our decision.

"Bring us the sparkling grape juice, please, Paulo." I said. Does it also have a special name?"

"Buta of course, my friends," he answered slyly. "It is called 'Raisin de Carbone.' We even add our own label." He pronounced it 'ray-SEEN-day-car-bo-NAY.'

Leon and I were carefully taking mental notes of these names so that we could appear knowledgeable to the girls when the food arrived. Paulo left just as the girls returned. "Well, fellas, what did you order?" asked Phyllis.

"It's a surprise," announced Leon. "And it was Joey's idea. I think you're going to like it." That left Leon covered. He had prepared them for the best, but in case the meal didn't live up to expectations, I would receive all the credit (blame).

I decided to change the subject. I was getting credit for too many things for one day and I was bound to draw a loser soon. "Hey, Leon," I asked, "what was that business about there not being fish on the menu?"

Phyllis and Leon started laughing. Erica's puzzled look must have matched mine. "Every time we go to a decent restaurant to eat," said Phyllis, "Leon looks to see if there is fish on the menu. He keeps threatening to do what one of his classmates at school does. It's really crazy. Go on, Leon. Tell them about Squeaky."

"Sure, why not," agreed Leon. "Joey, you're probably going to think all the people I know are strange. The guy we're talking about is *not* a friend of mine, but he is in my class at school and everyone knows him. His name is Ted Donaldson, but everyone calls him Squeaky because he is such a cheapskate. They claim that he holds onto money so tight that it squeaks when he lets go. Anyway, he started dating the most absolutely beautiful girls as soon as he got his driver's license. Since he's nothing special either in appearance or in personality, we were trying to figure out how he was doing it."

"Hey," said Phyllis "what are we if not the most beautiful girls you've ever seen?"

I wanted to see Leon get out of this one. "Okay, let me make this distinction," stammered Leon. "They are tier 2 girls and you two are tier 1 girls. In fact you are the only two in tier 1." *Nice save, Leon*, I thought.

"Thank you for clearing that up," said Phyllis. Erica just smiled at me and squeezed my arm. I mouthed a silent "It's true!" to her.

"Anyway, back to my story. Now where was I? Oh, yeah, then we found out that none of the girls would ever go out with him again.

One date and that was all. And the girls were from schools all over the city, never two from the same school. We finally got the story about Squeaky's successes and failures from one of his most recent dates about two months ago. It seems that he would go to dances at various high schools around the city. While there he would look for the prettiest girl, dance with her a couple of times, and invite her out to dinner at a nice restaurant a week later. He went to all the best spots. We couldn't figure that out since he was so cheap. The girl explained it this way.

"He would take the girl to a fancy restaurant and he would always order fish. Then he would encourage the girl to order something expensive, you know, like lobster or filet mignon. About three bites into his meal he would start coughing and then choking. This of course got the immediate attention of their waiter and usually the manager. He would then appear to remove a fish bone from his mouth and stare at it in disbelief. The manager would always make deepest apologies, offer to replace the fish with the best steak in the house, and would tear up the bill. Of course Squeaky would always leave the waiter a tip, but half the time the waiter would insist he take it back. It apparently did not take much insisting. It seems that Squeaky always carried his own fish bone into the restaurant just in case the chef did not conveniently leave a bone in the fish that was ordered.

"Now Squeaky's no dummy. He never went to the same restaurant twice. Apparently, though, he had not covered all the bases. The girl that gave us the story was with him the night he ran into a chef for the second time. I guess it was a pretty wild night.

"He pulled his usual routine and the waiter and the manager made the usual offer when the chef came out of the kitchen to see what was going on. This chef had just switched jobs from one of the other places where Squeaky had pulled the same routine. The chef recognized Squeaky, grabbed the bone from him, and started yelling something about the fish being a walleyed pike and the bone was from a perch. Then he reached into his apron and pulled out a meat cleaver and lit out after Squeaky. The manager told them to get out while he calmed down the chef. They took off and she hasn't seen Squeaky since, which is fine with her."

It was one of the wildest stories I'd ever heard, but after meeting RG3 and Mad Dog Norkus, and hearing about Homer Sweet, I wasn't surprised by it. Erica and I both had a good laugh over that one. I'd have to remember the story. It was a good one to tell while waiting for your food to arrive.

Speaking of the arrival of food, Paulo brought our order just as we were settling down after Leon's story. He served the food with a flourish. "These gentlemen surprisa me, ladies," he said in a most serious but complimentary tone. "Thisa is such a speciala dish that we make it only upona request. It doesa not even appear ona our menu. Your friends know the best of Italian food." He placed a steaming dish in front of Erica and Phyllis before serving Leon and me. Then he poured the sparkling grape juice into champagne glasses. The girls certainly seemed to be impressed. He then placed the half-empty bottle in what looked like an ice bucket on stilts, which was in front of the table but within my reach. Then he smiled at us, bowed, and left.

"It looks delicious," said Erica, carefully tasting the contents of the dish. "Oh! This is sinfully good. What is it called?"

"It's called Calizzo," I said, proud of my pronunciation. "I find there are very few places that even know what it is."

"Now come on, guys," Phyllis said. "This can't be champagne. I'm sure they wouldn't sell us anything alcoholic, but it does taste a little like champagne. What is it, Leon?"

"It's a dry, sparkling grape juice called Raisin de Carbone," he said, butchering the pronunciation. "Paulo suggested it when I asked if he had anything special to go with our food. You know, this place really is nice. Thanks for suggesting it, Erica."

We thoroughly enjoyed our meal and the leisurely but cozy atmosphere. When Paulo brought the bill we were prepared to be broke the rest of the week, but the price was very reasonable. Obviously Paulo survived on large tips and we felt that he certainly deserved one. We figured a normal tip and then doubled it.

Soon we were back in the car and heading for home. Leon had agreed to find a long way home but refused to take my suggestion of returning home by way of Milwaukee. Erica had again taken up residence at my side with my arm around her and her head on my shoulder. Her hair still smelled fresh, and she had apparently added a touch of perfume before leaving Paulo's because I could catch traces of it periodically. It wasn't a heavy scent, just devastating. I began to wonder how many senses you could lose and still enjoy a date as much as I was enjoying this one. I wondered if the girls of Chicago in general, and Erica in particular, had the same rules as the Benton Harbor girls about kissing. Back home the rule was "no kisses until the third date," and I didn't often make it to a third date.

Sensing that I needed all the time I could get, Leon dropped Phyllis off first. He was gone about ten minutes saying his good-byes to Phyllis. While we were sitting in the car waiting, I reached over and took Erica's left hand in my right hand. I squeezed it gently and she returned the pressure. "What are you feeling, Joey?" she asked without looking up. Her voice was soft, gentle, affectionate.

"I'm not very good about talking about my feelings," I said nervously, "but I was sort of wishing that tonight would never end. And if it had to end, then I want Thursday to hurry up and get here. But I don't want Thursday to ever end."

"Oh, Joey," she said sadly. "I feel the same way."

She looked up and our eyes locked. I felt like I was seeing something well below the surface for the first time. Her eyes appeared to be very moist. Her hair brushed against my hand and felt soft and sensuous. Our faces moved toward a common point where our lips met. Time stood still; breathing was unnecessary. I think God teases us with short glimpses of heaven to make us realize that heaven is ultimately where we belong.

Our lips parted and I was quite sure the ten-second rule had been violated by a few seconds. I hate it when those kinds of thoughts creep in at moments like this.

Erica had just put her head back on my shoulder when Leon reentered the car. Her hand was still in mine while my other hand stroked her hair. We drove in silence to Erica's house. Reluctantly I left the car with her and we walked slowly, hand in hand, to her door. "Call me tomorrow, Joey?" she asked.

"Try to stop me," I said, smiling at her. "Would four o'clock be okay?"

"I'll be waiting," she said as she put her arms around my neck and drew close to me. I hugged her wishing for time to stand still again. We kissed again before she turned and unlocked the door and entered the house. I walked back to the car slowly as heaven faded behind me and the chill of the night air enveloped me. With the chill I became aware of dampness on my shirt where Erica's head had rested. Had she been crying?

CHAPTER 26

The Dilemma

Upon awakening Wednesday morning, I found the clouds and rain of the previous day had been supplanted by warm sunshine and a pleasant breeze. My feelings, however, were in disarray. I was elated by the events of the previous evening, but I was confused by Erica's tears. What could they possibly mean?

I had spent a fitful night punctuated by short periods of sleep. Leon's snoring again reared its ugly head. In addition to trying to decipher Erica's concerns, I had my own as well. I like Erica very much and I knew I wanted to get to know her better, but I had no idea how to carry on a long-distance relationship. I knew her tears were not the result of not liking me. She had said things she didn't need to say with a sincerity that was not faked. The way she held my hand and snuggled close to me and the way she responded to our kisses made it clear how she felt about me. And I'm sure she could sense that my response was equally as sincere and strong.

Maybe she had another boyfriend. That would be understandable but the thought frightened me. How could I hope to compete with someone she could see every day? I was beginning to hope that she was concerned, as I was, about a long-distance relationship. This, at least, was where our concerns could merge and I gave this a great deal of thought.

First of all, not seeing each other all the time could be a good thing. I was certainly planning to go to college and I got the impression that she was too. Therefore, we had plenty of time to establish a serious relationship if that is what we both wanted. Of course it would be important to see each other at least occasionally. Fortunately, Chicago and Benton Harbor were well connected by both bus and train. I knew I could get to Chicago and I even had a place to stay. I wondered if Erica's parents would let her travel to Benton Harbor. She was at the top of my list as someone I would like to take to our homecoming dance in October and our prom in May. In fact, she was the only one on my list.

I suppose that the rest of the time we could write to one another. Phone calls were not likely because long distance call charges[2] were quite high. If a ten-dollar charge showed up on our phone bill, my parents would go through the roof.

---

2   For today's young people, a bit of history. Back in 1960 there were no cell phones. Most home phones had a rotary dial and all had cords, often long cords that became hopelessly twisted. Long distance calls were charged by the minute depending on the distance between the place called and the call's origin. These charges added up fast. If you were calling from a pay phone, you usually lined up several dollars in change, mostly quarters, and an operator interrupted your call periodically to have you deposit more coins. When you ran out of coins, your call was over. I know it's primitive but that's what we had.

CHAPTER 27

Chores and Distractions

I was trying to decide whether to stay in bed and think or get up and have breakfast, when Leon awoke, sat straight up, threw his legs over the side of the bed, stretched, yawned, and shook his head vigorously. Some things in life are constants. He then looked out the window. "Darn!" he said. "Why couldn't it rain today instead of yesterday?" He seemed genuinely disappointed.

"What's so special about today?" I asked.

"Today is the day I have to cut the grass, trim the hedges, weed the flower garden and almost everything else around here except shingle the roof," complained Leon with disgust.

"It can't be any worse than our yard," I responded. "I'll help you. It won't take all that long."

After breakfast, Leon and I went out to the yard to survey the job. There was only one lawn mower and Leon was familiar with its idiosyncrasies, so he cut the grass while I started weeding the flower garden. Cindy came out and wanted to talk so she helped me with the garden.

"You'll never guess what happened to Frieda last night. Apparently Leon was very upset by the things she tried to pull on you Monday night and he complained to Dad about her. Dad sat her down after you and Leon went out last night and had a little heart-to-heart with her except that he did all the talking and she did all the listening. After that, she just left the family room and went and ironed the shirts from the laundry without being told. She was really quiet the rest of the night. Apparently Dad listed all of the things she had done to you since you arrived and I'm guessing he didn't miss much. It may be peaceful around here for the rest of the week. By the way, how did your date with Erica go?"

"We had a wonderful time except that at the end of the evening she seemed saddened by something. I can't figure out what it was," I replied.

Cindy looked a little pensive for a moment and then said, "Oh, it's probably nothing. Try not to worry about it." Then, changing the subject, she asked, "What are you doing this afternoon, Joey?"

"Well, Leon said something about another rehearsal before tomorrow night's job. I'll probably go over to Frank's house with Leon and watch another rehearsal," I said. "Why? Is there something else going on?"

"Maybe," she said. "I was just talking to Jennie. She's one of my friends from school. Anyway, she's trying to get a group of people together to play softball this afternoon. Most of them will probably be girls, but there are usually a few boys that play too. I didn't think being outnumbered by girls was against your religion, so I figured you might want to go. We'd love to have you. How about it?"

How could a normal teenage boy say no to Cindy? Besides, I had already seen ELF's entire act for their Thursday job. "I think I will go, Cindy," I responded enthusiastically. "Maybe I'll even sign autographs afterward."

"I don't know about that," she said coyly. "You may want to collect a few, along with phone numbers. I don't mind telling you that I have some very pretty friends."

"They can't be any prettier than you," I said with conviction. "But I'll be happy to check them out and give you an outsider's opinion." It was unlikely that I would try to get any phone numbers. My dance card was already full with Erica. But a distraction is a distraction and I needed one right now.

"Be ready by one o'clock," Cindy said as she scampered back into the house. There was a hint of a blush on her cheeks.

CHAPTER 28

The Softball Game

A few minutes past one o'clock found Leon backing the Plymouth into the street, guitar case in the backseat, to go to Frank's house for the final ELF rehearsal before becoming professionals. At the same time, I left the house with Cindy. I had Uncle Fred's softball glove since he was also left-handed. If it weren't for our advanced intelligence, being left-handed would really be a sad situation. So few things are made for left-handed people. We almost always have to adapt to devices designed by and for right-handed people. Of course, we can usually do this. Thus my claim, supported by Uncle Fred, to intellectual superiority. Have you ever watched a right-handed person try to learn to use something designed for a left-handed person? It is really a pathetic sight. They are usually reduced to tears.

We, however, were far from tears. Cindy was her usual playful self. She would drop her glove and then tickle me when I bent down to pick it up. When I attempted to retaliate, she would run ahead and turn to laugh when she was out of reach. My sisters used to do things like that and it made me furious. I knew, of course, that they hated me. All I felt now was a little frustration at not being able to catch Cindy. She was just being playful. I decided to give pity a try. I sat down Indian-style on the sidewalk, rested my elbows on my knees, and hung my head in my hands. Cindy started back toward me, cautiously at first, and said,

"I'm sorry, Joey. I'll stop. Sometimes I'm such an awful tease. Will you forgive me?" She had reached the spot where I was sitting and had stooped down to be closer to me and to show me her sincerity.

That was her fatal mistake. "Okay," I said, trying to keep an offended look on my face. I extended my hands toward her, inviting her to help me up. She did. When I was on my feet, I pulled her firmly toward me and tickled her unmercifully.

"You scoundrel!' she shouted as she tried to fight me off. I decided I had better quit before she drew a crowd and I got in trouble. I backed away and raised my hands as a sign of truce. Cindy composed herself, walked over to me, and slipped her arm through mine. "I deserved that," she said and smiled. We continued on to the park where we were to meet the group. It was the same park where we had played basketball on Monday.

Several people were already there and more arrived just after Cindy and I. In all, there were sixteen people: twelve girls and four guys. It was easy enough to remember the other three guys, especially since one of them was Mad Dog Norkus. The other two guys were normal. Their names were Dan and Tom. They were both of average height and average weight, and I didn't think they were any better looking than I was. Not much of a challenge there. The girls, on the other hand, were six blonds (Carol, Tina, Anne, Wendy, Paula, and Cindy); four brunettes (Jennie, Tracie, Mary, and Kelly); and two redheads (Kay and Amber).

We chose up teams of eight and agreed that the batter would also act as catcher and toss the ball back to the pitcher. Of course there would be no stealing of bases. The pitcher would cover the plate after a hit. There would be no bunting. There were two guys on each team and they had to play in the outfield. I asked why that was and was told that guys playing the infield threw the ball too hard, and besides, they could get the ball in from the outfield more easily. I guess that made sense.

Jennie, Cindy's friend and the apparent organizer of the game, insisted that each team needed a name. Her team, of which I was a member, would henceforth be known as the Beachcombers. The other team, which included Cindy and Mad Dog, decided to call themselves the Base Jockeys.

The game began with the Beachcombers on the field and the Base Jockeys at bat. Jennie chose herself to be our pitcher and Kay, who could throw a ball an amazingly long way, played right field with Dan in left and me in center. Paula, a tall, slender, and graceful blond who was kind of pretty played first base. Mary played second base, Tina was shortstop, and Anne was at third. As I was staring at the combined beauty of our infield (and pitcher), I heard a feminine cry of "heads up!" from Kay and looked up just in time to see the ball she had thrown descend from the sky. In self-defense I caught the ball. I turned and threw the ball to Dan trying to make the whole process look as natural as possible. Dan had been similarly distracted and I had to holler a quick "heads up!" just before I threw the ball and afterward gave him an understanding nod.

Fortunately, before anything else could be thrown my way, Jennie called for the game to commence. The batter hit the first pitch to third, Anne scooped up the ball and threw it to first for the out. I was amazed. I didn't think girls could really catch a ball or really throw a ball. I figured that Kay was the exception. It turned out that all these girls played softball in both school and summer leagues. If all the girls who play softball were as pretty as these girls, I would have to look into coaching a team back home.

Play continued with our opponents making three consecutive outs. Jennie set our batting order and decided that Dan would lead off, Kay would bat next with Jennie third and me fourth. As Dan approached the plate we began to hear the unmistakable line of chatter from Mad Dog who was playing left field. Beth, who had possibly the cutest smile on the field (after Cindy), was pitching. She lobbed the first pitch in and Dan took a huge backswing in anticipation of a fat pitch. Just as the ball reached the plate, Beth said in a terribly sexy voice, "Hi, Danny." Dan uncorked his swing, missed the ball by a mile, and turned beet-red.

"I guess I should have expected that," said Jennie. "Dan is completely gone on Beth." Then she shouted to Dan, "Come on, Dan, hit the ball. Beth'll still talk to you after the game." Dan's face turned even redder, but he hit the next pitch to left field where it fell just in front of Mad Dog who had misjudged it and was running back. He made it to second base where Cindy almost tagged him out.

Kay hit the ball down the first base line, an easy out but Dan advanced to third. Jennie hit a long fly ball to Tom in center, which he caught, but Dan was able to tag up and score from third.

Now it was my turn at bat. The fences didn't look too far away and I figured that I should hit at least two out of the park this afternoon. The first pitch looked good and I took a gigantic swing. I missed and nearly fell over. "Come on, Joey, get a hit," said Jennie joined by the rest of the team.

"No hitter," said Mad Dog from left. "He couldn't hit a watermelon with a fungo bat."

I took a mighty swing at the next pitch and missed again. This was embarrassing.

"Just take an easy swing and connect, Joey," said Jennie. "Don't try to kill the ball." I couldn't tell you how many times my dad and my coaches had told me the same thing. Maybe Jennie was right. I decided to swing easy on the next pitch and just try to meet the ball. Beth delivered the ball. It was outside. I let it go. The next pitch looked good. I waited, took a steady but easy swing, and connected. The ball flew off the bat, a line drive—right back to Beth. She made the catch for an easy out. The sun seemed to be getting hotter. Or maybe it was just the heat of everyone staring at me. Embarrassed, I looked around. Nobody was staring at me. They were just grabbing gloves and heading out to take the field. Kay jogged out toward me with my glove and smiled. "Good try, Joey. A couple of inches higher and it would have cleared the fence. Get it next time." She tossed my glove to me.

"Thanks," I said. "You know, you girls play a pretty good game of softball." I wanted to direct attention away from me.

"I think that's a compliment," Kay responded as we trotted to the outfield. "Anyway, thank you. We have a team at our school. I wish they would let us play baseball though. A baseball is easier to throw, and I can throw one a lot farther than a softball." We separated to move to our respective positions in the field. Kay called back over her shoulder, "You can buy me a coke after the game if you'd like." This was an incredible week, even with the shut-out at the beach on Sunday. These Chicago girls were not shy. I had already been approached positively by four girls so far this week and that brought my lifetime total to…four. I definitely needed to do more travelling.

Mad Dog was the first batter and he hit the first pitch over the fence in left field. I was impressed. He had more talent than I thought. What happened next, however, impressed me even more. As he toured the bases he stopped at each one, took the ungloved hand of each of the girls, and kissed it, then proceeded to the next base. At second base both Mary and Tina were waiting. Obviously this was common protocol with this group, at least where Mad Dog was concerned. He trotted on to Kelly at third and then on to home plate. Upon his arrival at home, all the girls on his team lined up and gave him a kiss. I hoped for two things. First, that this practice applied to any guy who hit a home run, and second, that I could get my swing straightened out.

There was no more scoring that inning for either side. The game was tied as we moved into the third inning of what was agreed to be a six-inning game. Our opponents scored three runs in their half of the third. In our half of the inning, our first two batters were walked and Dan hit a double to drive them in. Kay lined out to the shortstop and Jennie walked. It was my turn to bat again and I had resolved to swing a little easier and smoother. I fouled off the first pitch. The next pitch was perfect and I hit a fly ball between left and center field. Both Tom and Mad Dog ran for it, but it dropped just in front of them and rolled between them. Amazingly Mad Dog was the first one to the ball.

As I rounded first base it looked like he was fumbling with the ball so I took off for second base. Halfway to second base, I realized that Mad Dog had suckered me. He had full control of the ball and fired it to second base where Cindy had the ball and was waiting for me.

My choice was to run in standing up and get tagged out or to try to slide past Cindy and hook the bag with my foot on the way by. I slid. Cindy simply fell on top of me and put on the tag. About fourteen people yelled "Out!" and Cindy just rested on top of me for a few seconds, put her elbow on my chest and said, "You're getting kind of chummy with the redhead, aren't you?" Then she got up and walked off toward the bench.

Kay came by with my glove and helped me to my feet. "Nice hit, Joey," she said with a sexy smile. "I thought Mad Dog had fumbled it too. That cute little guy is always doing something like that. I guess that's why so many girls fuss over him."

We walked back to our positions and I called out to her as we separated. "Do you still want to go out for a coke after the game?" I asked, wondering if Cindy could hear me.

"I'm looking forward to it, Joey," she called back. I was having a difficult time keeping my mind on the game (the ball game, that is.)

At least my hit had driven in two runs before I was tagged out. We now led 5-4. Each team scored a run in the fourth inning and each team failed to score a run in the fifth inning. In the sixth inning, Mad Dog again hit a home run with the same results, kisses to all his opponent basewomen and kisses from all his female teammates. It must be a local custom for hitting a home run. Mad Dog couldn't possibly have that much charisma.

When Tom came to bat with two outs, it looked like he was going to try to get in on the act too. He hit a long fly ball to center field that looked like it was headed for the fence. I turned and raced toward the fence. I reached up and caught the ball as it passed over my shoulder. At the same moment, I hit the fence and flipped over it. For dramatic effect, I decided to lay on the other side of the fence until relief arrived. Kay and Dan were the first to get there. "Joey! Are you all right?" said Kay with concern. I could hear the others running out and shouting. I opened my eyes, smiled at Kay, and raised my right hand with the ball safely in the glove. "I caught it," I shouted. There were shouts of joy and cries of dismay depending on which team you heard. The walk in was very pleasant with teammates giving me handshakes and hugs of congratulations. I must admit, the girls' perfume was holding up pretty well considering the warm sun and the dust of six innings of ball.

Kay was our first batter and she beat out a grounder to shortstop for a single. Jennie flied out to right. This would be my last chance at a home run unless we played several extra innings. The score was tied at 6-6. I stood at the plate waiting for the pitch trying not to appear nervous. Beth was still pitching and got me to foul off the first two pitches. The next two pitches were outside. I stepped out of the batter's box and tried to relax. I couldn't figure out why this seemed to mean so much to me. Everybody else was just trying to have fun, but I seemed to have to prove something. The pressure just wasn't worth it. This time next week, I'd be back home and everybody here would probably have forgotten about me. What the heck.

I stepped back in. Beth delivered a pitch right down the middle, and I took an even, relaxed swing at the ball. It didn't feel like much of a swing, but I must have made perfectly timed contact because the ball flew off the bat and headed for the right-center field fence. The outfielders didn't even try for it. I made the trip around the bases, stopping to kiss the hands of Tracie, Cindy, Amber, and Kelly.

When I approached home I was not disappointed. The line had already formed. Dan was in front and fortunately offered only a handshake. Next was Jennie with an enthusiastic kiss and hug. I continued to make my way down the line in no particular hurry. This was better than food. Kay was at the end of the line and it looked like she had dug in. She hung on real good and planted a kiss that probably registered on the University of Chicago's seismograph. What a way to contribute to scientific research.

CHAPTER 29

Thank You, Mad Dog

After the game, we all went to the SUNDAE SHOPPE for cokes. Once there, it was interesting to watch the groups form. Dan and Beth went off to a booth. Tom and Wendy paired off and found a small table. I was joined in a booth by Kay on one side and Jennie and Cindy on the other. The other seven girls crowded into a large booth toward the back with Mad Dog. He was loving every minute of it. Of course, I wasn't complaining. Jennie, Cindy, and Kay were three of the cutest girls there and Kay sure knew how to maintain a guy's interest. This was one team picture I sure would like to take home with me. My classmates would never believe me.

We drank cokes and talked for about an hour. I was really having a good time, forgetting for a while that I would be leaving on Friday and also forgetting about the party with Erica on Thursday. It seemed like, for now at least, this was where I belonged. Finally things started to break up. Dan and Beth were the first to leave, followed soon after by Tom and Wendy. Each stopped by our table and said their good-byes. Just before we were to leave, I got up to use the restroom and was followed by Mad Dog.

"Hey, Joey," he said as we were washing our hands. "Could you loan me a dollar? I guess I got more popularity than I can afford."

"Sure, Mad Dog," I said, pulling out my wallet. "How do you do it anyway? I'd sure like to know your secret."

"It's no secret, Joey," he said, taking the dollar I offered. "Just don't try to be something you're not. I'm goofy so I don't try to be cool. Just be honest. You seem to do a pretty good job of that."

It made sense, especially if you were goofy. At least that could be entertaining. I guess the first thing you have to do is figure out who you are and accept it. I still wasn't sure who I was so the only thing I could be honest about was uncertainty. But that was something.

"By the way, Joey, have you heard from Erica lately?" asked Mad Dog as we left the restroom. "I was kind of hoping she would be at the ball game. She's really a sharp-looking chick."

"Omigosh!" I exclaimed. "What time is it? I was supposed to call her at four o'clock."

"You're out of luck, Joey," said Mad Dog with a sly grin. "My watch says four-oh-four. It's a good thing this place has a pay phone. I hope you have a dime."

I spotted the phone about halfway down the corridor, which led to the fountain area. I fished in my pocket, found enough change to make the call, and dialed Erica's number.

"Hello, Andersens' residence, Erica speaking."

"Hi, Erica. It's me, Joey."

"I just knew it would be you, Joey. I even won a bet with my mother. She told me not to be upset if you forgot or called late. She says that very few guys are so dependable that they always call when they say they will. But I told her you were different."

I felt really rotten that I had nearly forgotten to call. In fact, it was only Mad Dog's off-hand reference to Erica that reminded me. I didn't have the courage to tell Erica the truth right then. I did, however, plan to be honest with her about it tomorrow when I saw her and we could talk face-to-face. "How could any guy forget to call you, Erica?" I asked. Actually, it was a completely sincere question, notwithstanding the fact that I had forgotten. "Besides, I intentionally forgot to ask you what time the party would start so I would have an excuse to call."

"You know, I intentionally forgot to tell you when the party would start so you'd have to call me," she said.

"Speaking of the party," I said, "when does it begin?"

"I'm glad you thought to ask," she responded, continuing the charade. "I'll pick you up at about ten after six if that's okay. The problem is that I don't know when the party will be over. Amy, she's the one giving the party, was pretty vague about when the party would end. My parents will probably set a curfew though."

"I'll be ready. Maybe Uncle Fred will give me a key in case I'm late. I'm sure looking forward to tomorrow night."

"So am I," said Erica sincerely. "Say, where are you calling from? It sounds kind of noisy."

"Oh, I'm at the SUNDAE SHOPPE with Cindy and a bunch of her friends. We just finished playing a softball game. I'll bet you wish you were here. Mad Dog Norkus is sitting in a booth not twenty feet from me, surrounded by girls."

"Oh, darn," said Erica. "That Mad Dog is so cute too. Say, was that game organized by a girl named Jennie?"

"As a matter of fact, it was. How did you know?"

"Mom said she called late this morning while I was at the grocery store picking up milk and bread. Now I am disappointed. I guess I better let you go."

"See you tomorrow at six-ten, Erica," I said and put the receiver down.

Outside, just before we went our separate ways home, I jokingly offered to give each girl a hug and a kiss, seeing as how I'd be going home Friday and might not ever see them again. To my surprise, they all took me up on the offer, even Cindy. Again, Kay was a little more enthusiastic than the rest, but nobody acted as though they were doing me a huge favor. Maybe I had a future as a dirty old man.

Cindy and I started toward home. For a block or so we were quiet, enjoying the experience we'd just had. Finally I said, "Cindy, you sure have an interesting group of friends. I don't think I've ever seen so many pretty girls all together in one place. I have to admit, though, I think you're still the prettiest one of the group."

Cindy blushed and then replied, "Thank you, Joey. I think you really mean it." Then after thinking for a minute she said, "You sure had trouble taking your eyes off of Kay."

Now I think I started to blush. "Well, she's pretty too, and she isn't my cousin. Does she show that much interest in every guy?"

"Almost," answered Cindy. "She's probably the biggest flirt in Illinois. Not that she isn't nice. She is. She just loves to flirt with boys. I do think she liked you, though."

"Darn," I said, "and I forgot to get her address and phone number."

Cindy reached in her purse and handed me a slip of paper. "She had me write it down for you while you were in the back with Mad Dog." Then she added, "You know of course that we are not blood-related cousins, just cousins by marriage. Right?"

CHAPTER 30

Uncle Fred's Surprise

Cindy and I arrived home just as Uncle Fred drove into the garage. "Hi, kids!" he said with a bright smile. "Guess what I got at work today?"

"Gee, Dad," said Cindy, "did you get a raise?"

"Cindy, Cindy, Cindy," chided Uncle Fred, "how many times do I need to remind you that I own the company. Every time I get new business, I get a raise. And any time I lose business I take a pay cut." Then he smiled and said, "But I did get a string of complimentary tickets to Riverview and I thought that you, Joey, and Leon might like to go tonight. How about it?"

"Oh wow, Dad!" shouted Cindy. "Thanks. Oh, Joey, this is really going to be fun. You know about Riverview, don't you?"

"Sure," I said. "It's an amusement park. I see ads for it all the time on TV. I've never been there but I've always wanted to go. Thanks, Uncle Fred."

We ran into the house to find Leon and tell him. Our first guess was correct. He was watching TV. "Leon!" said Cindy. "Dad got a whole string of complimentary tickets to Riverview for you, Joey, and me to use tonight. He also gave us some money and told us to get supper at the park or on the way home. Isn't that neat?"

"Oh, sure! You guys get to go to Riverview and I suppose I have to sit home and rot." It was Frieda. I hadn't even noticed her. She was curled up in the corner sitting behind a stack of floor cushions. "Dad knows I'm grounded, but he goes ahead and gets tickets for you guys. I hate being the youngest. Everybody always picks on me and nobody ever gets anything good for me. They might just as well take me out in the backyard and shoot me." She got up and stormed out of the room, stopping at the doorway to say, "I hope the parachute rips for all of you on the parachute drop."

"Boy, do I ever feel cursed," I said to Cindy and Leon in mock despair. "Maybe we better stay home. Did Uncle Fred and Aunt Leona buy her from a band of gypsies? Even my little sister isn't that big a brat." I ran and jumped behind the cushions and pulled a few over on top of me in an effort to protect myself. "Do her curses penetrate sturdy floor cushions?" I shouted out.

Cindy and Leon doubled up with laughter. "Relax," said Leon. "The only thing that ever died around here was her goldfish and it committed suicide by jumping out of the bowl. Besides, Cindy is the only one who likes the parachute drop. I could manage around here if her 'chute failed."

Cindy grabbed one of the pillows covering me and threw it at Leon. "Leon's just chicken. He's afraid of the parachute drop and the roller coasters. Besides, Leon, maybe Joey would like to go on those rides with me. How about it, Joey? Sometimes I need someone strong to hang on to." She stared at me with a look of feigned dependence in her large, sky-blue eyes and a slight, pleading pout on her lips.

Leon jumped in. "I am not afraid of the parachute drop. I'm just thinking ahead and keeping my options open. I've heard that when you get drafted into the army, they ask you if you've done the parachute drop at Riverview and if you like roller coasters. They're always looking for paratroopers and fighter pilots. So there." Cindy was probably right; Leon was chicken.

I usually don't like roller coasters, but if Cindy was going to hang onto me, I figured I could sacrifice myself for her protection. I had always been interested in airplanes and anything related to them. I wondered what it would be like to make a parachute jump. "Don't worry, Cindy," I said as I put my arm around her shoulder. "I'll go with you on any ride you want."

"Oh brother!" said Leon disgustedly. "We aren't even there and I'm ready to throw up."

We looked at each other and laughed. "Let's go upstairs and get cleaned up and change clothes," said Cindy. "Then we can take off. Do you guys want to eat before or after the park?"

"Afterward," replied Leon. "I don't think I want to face some of those rides on a full stomach."

We all laughed again and went upstairs to get ready. I was kind of hoping that Cindy was serious about hanging onto me during the rides.

CHAPTER 31

First Lessons at Riverview

We arrived at the park at about six-thirty. It looked busy with lots of people and the rides were seemingly in constant motion. There were screams coming from different directions as other people were hawking the various attractions. I stopped for a moment as we waited in line at the entrance to the park. I tried to take it all in at once. Every time I try to do that with a scene like this, sounds start to blur and objects distort. Small objects seem to get larger and large objects seem to get smaller. The sounds blend and then blur again. It's like listening to Stravinski run amok with the turntable alternately speeding up and slowing down but rarely playing at the correct speed and adding corresponding visuals. I can remember that as a kid I used to have nightmares like that, but when you do it fully awake, it is really weird.

I must have looked strange because all of a sudden somebody was shaking me and I heard Cindy calling to me from a distance. "Joey. Are you okay? Joey?"

Her voice came closer as the scene in my mind disappeared. She was right next to me with a concerned look on her face. I smiled at her. "I'm fine, Cindy. I just do this daydreaming thing sometimes, and I guess I must look pretty strange when I do it." I went on and tried to explain it to her and Leon as we entered the park. I even tried to teach them how to do it but I guess it didn't work for them. Or maybe it scared them and they didn't really try. And I thought everyone could do it. "Gee," said Leon, "I wish I could do it. It sounds like having your own amusement ride in your brain. Oh, well, who's going to be the first one to ride the Scrambler?"

"I will," yelled Cindy as she ran on ahead, "'cause I've got the tickets."

"I guess Cindy wins that round," I said, "right, Leon?" Leon just shrugged his shoulders in defeat as we ran to catch up to Cindy.

The Scrambler was an interesting-looking ride, which had four arms extending out from the center. On each arm there were four compartments each having seating space for two or three people. The whole device would spin around and then the compartments on each arm would also rotate. I imagined the dizziness this double rotation could cause and had second thoughts. Then I remembered my promise to Cindy and joined her in line along with Leon. There was only a short wait before it was our turn to find seats on the ride. Leon decided to let us have one compartment to ourselves while he shared one with a cute blond who seemed to be alone and also seemed not to mind having a companion. After everyone was seated, an attendant came around and made sure the safety bar was securely in place and then flipped a switch to start the ride. It started out tame enough. Realizing, however, the effect of centrifugal force, I lifted my arm onto the back of our seat and waited for Cindy to slide toward me as the ride pick up speed. The ride did gain speed, Cindy did slide over to press tightly against me and I did offer a prayer of thanksgiving for the wonders of applied physics. (That's why I chose the outside seat.)

The ride slowed down all too soon, although Cindy remained huddled close to me until the attendant came by and released the bar. "I love this ride, Joey," she said delightedly. "Let's come back to it later."

"Whenever you want to, Cindy," I said agreeably. "This is a fun ride. Where to next?"

"Hey, guys, wait up!" It was Leon. Or maybe I should say it was Leon with a minor goddess on his arm. As they got closer, I could see that she was much prettier than she had appeared as she sat in the compartment next to Leon some distance away from us. She appeared to be several inches taller than me but much shorter than Leon. Her golden blond hair worn in a pageboy style, striking gray eyes, and a delicately sculpted face were all highlighted by a most attractive smile. Her skin was lightly tanned and her body looked like a Greek statue, the dainty ones, not the chubby ones. "This is Lois. I'm rescuing her. If she comes with me, she doesn't have to stay with her dad and little sister."

"Hi, Lois," I said. "I'm Joey, Leon's cousin and this is his sister Cindy." I was impressed with Leon. He seemed to figure that you get the girl first, regardless of the reason, then you figure out how to keep her. I couldn't help wondering if she was more interested in getting away from her little sister than she was in being with Leon. Anyway, that was Leon's problem.

"Hi, Joey. Hi Cindy," she said in a completely uncharacteristic high-pitched voice. It was like seeing John Wayne on the screen but hearing the voice of Daffy Duck.

"Cindy, could you give me some of the tickets?" asked Leon. "You guys can take the rest and I'll meet you at the park entrance gate at closing time. Please?"

"Here Leon," said Cindy. "You've got some money, don't you?" Leon nodded. "Good. Take off, we'll see you later."

Leon grabbed the tickets and Lois's hand and was off with his new-found friend. "He wouldn't want to go on any of the same rides we do, anyway," said Cindy. "We'll have more fun and I know he will too. I wonder if he'll tell Phyllis about Lois?" she added, knowing he wouldn't.

"She is awfully cute," I observed, "but I couldn't believe her voice. Didn't you think it was strange?"

"Yeah, it was," agreed Cindy, "but I think it is wonderful that she is as pretty as she is and is able to be as confident as she is with that voice. If she overlooks it, probably others will too. Leon sure did. I think that's neat."

"You know, you're right," I replied. "I never thought about it that way. I guess no matter how perfect a person seems, there is always some imperfection to deal with. Everyone, that is, except Erica and you. And maybe Kay." Cindy smiled and blushed. "Maybe it's how we deal with the imperfections that makes us attractive to others."

"Gee, Joey," said Cindy with amazement. "I never expected a guy to understand that. You're right, you know." Then changing the subject, she grabbed my hand and said, "Let's try the nearest roller coaster."

We followed our ears to the nearest screams and there it was. It looked frightening. Back home there was a place called Silver Beach, which was a small amusement park in St. Joseph. It had one roller coaster that looked like a pygmy compared to this one. Cindy led on with enthusiasm. "The kids call this one 'Lunch's Rerun,'" she said with glee. I think I may have discovered Cindy's lone imperfection; she was demented. I began to wonder who would hold onto who on this one, but I followed gamely, trying to keep a smile on my face and giving the impression that I found this exciting.

We were seated in the front seat of the first car, which meant that we were sure to see our fate before falling prey to it. There was a seat belt, which went across both our laps. After that, there was a sliding bar that swung toward us and locked into place fractions of an inch from our belt. I embedded my fingers into the metal bar, but I kept the smile on my face. The cars began their slow ascent to the top of the first drop. I began to wonder if it was possible for the car to gain so much speed going down the hill that it would fly off the track. The mechanism below the car clanked insufferably, straining to move the cars to the top and for us, certain death.

As we reached the top I looked tentatively ahead. In shock I noticed that the track disappeared. There was no track until we hit bottom; at least I couldn't see any. I was terrified. We started down the steep decline, slowly at first but gathering speed until we were going at least 430 miles per hour. Girls behind us screamed. Some guy behind us said "I'm going to puke!" and it sounded like he meant it. My stomach got out and notified me that it was walking the rest of the way. I wondered how long I would have to hold my breath before I would lose consciousness. The car finally hit bottom but I didn't.

"That was neat, wasn't it, Joey?" stated Cindy, clinging to me.

Unable to fully appreciate her proximity, I said as bravely as a man with no stomach could, "Yeah. Is it over yet?"

"No, silly," she said. "That was just the first drop. There are eight more."

"Is that all?" I said, wishing I had written a will. "I think this one is over-rated. It's a sissy roller coaster. Let's get out now and try to find a real roller coaster."

At that moment we reached the top of the next drop and down we went. I grabbed Cindy like a drowning man grabs a life ring. "Hang on, kid," I said. "I'll protect you." I was glad that we had decided to eat afterward instead of before. Next the car went through a series of relatively small hills and valleys and then started back up a hill that made the first one look like a beginner's slope. I was convinced that we would reach the top, someone would stop the ride and demand that we give them all the money we had or they would drop us down to a slow, painful death. I was prepared to give them everything including my watch and class ring.

We reached the top. I looked in vain for the highwayman. Again the track disappeared. We started down. I felt myself fall forward. I was convinced that the bar and the seat belt had been mysteriously removed and I wondered what the priest would say at my funeral. The car leveled off and I gave a sigh of relief. Too soon. Again the earth dropped away and we were free falling. We finally hit bottom and the car quickly climbed a short rise and shot full speed into a spiral that got tighter and tighter.

All of a sudden we were on a length of straight track and we shuddered to a stop. I raised my eye lids hoping that my eyes were still behind them. They were. I could see. I saw my fingerprints permanently embedded in the safety bar as I disembarked from the car and helped Cindy out, wondering why the platform was so wobbly. A preacher who was serious about making converts could do a thriving business on that platform. "Gee, Cindy," I said, "that was fun. Now what?"

"Let's do the Ferris wheel first," she said exuberantly, "and then we can do the parachute drop. Come on!" She grabbed my hand and off we went. I like Ferris wheels and I hoped that the earthquake I felt as I walked along (nobody else seemed to notice) would subside by the time we got off the ride.

The one problem with the Ferris wheel is that it takes a long time to get it loaded. We were the first ones onto the ride so we moved only about halfway to the top before the wheel was stopped to reload the next car. Since the wheel wasn't fully occupied and there was not a long line waiting, they had to balance the load on the wheel as well. While we were waiting at the top of the wheel I leaned forward to look down. Naturally the car tipped forward but we were securely strapped in, so I wasn't worried. All of a sudden I heard a short scream beside me and Cindy clutched at my arm so tightly I was afraid it might have to be amputated. "Don't do that!" she screamed.

"What's the matter, Cindy?" I asked. "We're strapped in pretty tight. We won't fall out."

"I don't know why, Joey," she said as her face paled, "but I just get terrified when these chairs rock this high off the ground. I like the ride when it's going around, but I can't stand it when we stop at the top and rock. Please, Joey! Make it stop rocking."

I leaned back in an attempt to stabilize the chair. Now the only thing making the chair rock was Cindy. "Come here, Cindy. Just sit back and relax and the chair will stop rocking." She sat back and crushed in real close as I lifted my arm and put it around her shoulder. She felt like a lump of rock at that moment but smelled much nicer. She was so tense. "Relax, Cindy. The chair's not rocking anymore." She tried to relax but was not completely successful until the ride started up again. A couple of more stops and we were making continuous revolutions with a slight breeze blowing Cindy's hair against my cheek. She felt much softer and very feminine now. Her hair was soft and sweet smelling. And I was quickly forgetting the roller coaster.

The ride ended, and mercifully for Cindy, we were the first ones off. She had calmed down considerably but was still a bit rattled by the rocking incident at the top of the wheel. We walked around for a while before going to the parachute ride. I was looking forward to it and Cindy said that she always enjoyed it. "How come you can handle a parachute drop and rocking in a chair into which you are securely strapped terrifies you?" I asked.

"I'm not sure, Joey," she said. "Maybe it's because in a parachute you're supposed to drop and in a Ferris wheel chair you're not supposed to have that feeling. Anyway, on the Ferris wheel you don't have a parachute in case you fall out."

"I can't argue with that." I chuckled.

We worked our way to the front of the line for the parachute drop, turned in our tickets, and were fastened into the harness. Side by side we rose to the top of the superstructure and were released to float down to the ground. Now I had seen parachute drops on TV hundreds of times. The paratroopers always floated to the ground. I expected that, when we were released at the top, we could float lazily to the ground.

What actually happened when we were released is that there was a short period of free-fall while the parachute filled with air. I had not expected that. During that period of free-fall, which reminded me altogether too much of the roller coaster ride, I became convinced that my 'chute had failed and I was about to die. Praying faster than I thought possible, I was about two-thirds of the way through the act of contrition when my parachute filled with air, savagely jerking me from the grasp of free-fall, and I drifted lazily down to the ground.

My stomach rejoined me about twenty seconds later as I was being assisted out of the harness by an attendant who, with a shave and haircut, could play the part of King Kong. He was chewing (with greatly discolored teeth) on an unlit cigar and emitting breath that could double as paint remover. "Enjoy yer day," he ordered, "and don't throw up inside the fence." Compliance was fear-driven.

It was this experience more than any other that caused me to make a change in career plans from test pilot to an envelope licker in a ground floor office where all chairs had seat belts. I began to realize that I loved the thought of flying gracefully through the air but that there were too many airplane maneuvers that resembled free-fall, and free-fall sent me into shock.

Cindy was exuberant as she jumped unassisted out of the harness and ran over to me. Her nose wrinkled a bit as Kong walked by, audibly fouling the air as he passed. Then she smiled, grabbed my hand and said, "That was fun. Let's do it again before we leave."

"Sure, Cindy." I tried to be chivalrous even though the thought of repeating some of the rides frightened me. "Any ride you want. Why don't we try a few tame ones for a while so the exciting ones will be even more exciting?" *And I'll have a chance to recover*, I thought.

"Let's, Joey. I could use a breather anyway. Besides, some of the slower rides are fun too. Come on, let's find the bumper cars."

Off we went in search of the bumper cars. I had been on bumper cars at Silver Beach back home, and they were fun. I especially liked them when I was younger because it was as close as I could get to driving a car until I got a license. I remember that one time, when I was in about sixth grade, I actually tried to drive a bumper car for the whole time without hitting anything, just to impress my parents with how good a driver I was. Two years later, some of the guys in my class had a contest to see how many collisions they could instigate during the three-minute ride. I imagine parents would be pretty upset at the direction taken in priorities by the young male mind.

We found the ride and got into separate cars. We started out in opposite directions, each making numerous contacts with adjacent cars as we moved toward the middle of the floor where all the action took place. I lost sight of Cindy as I was bumped around in the center, and just as I was regaining control of my car and achieving a good attack position, I felt a strong jolt from behind. It was Cindy.

Usually it is pretty hard to make a solid hit on another car because you need to get a good run at them without interference. I looked around in surprise. Cindy laughed, backed up, and hit me again and again. So the battle was on, I thought. I tried to back away from her but she still hit me a glancing blow on the front right. As she backed up for another assault, I waited until she began her forward movement. Just before she reached me, I spun the wheel sharply to the left, causing my car to make a 360-degree spin. I slammed into her left side as she passed the position where I had been. Now I was on the attack. I backed up to make a run at her. She was trapped between two other cars and could go nowhere. I took aim, pushed the accelerator to the floor and…nothing happened. The ride was over. Oh, well!

We jumped out of the cars and walked to the exit, laughing as we relived the last couple of minutes. She took my hand as we walked. At first this bothered me a little because she was my cousin. But then I figured that if it didn't bother her, why should it bother me?

We rode on several more of the subdued rides and looked at various other attractions. We were having a good time and I was really enjoying Cindy's company—not so much like she was a date, but more like she was a fun person to be with. If she weren't my cousin, I probably would want to take her out. I also felt a little guilty that I didn't feel more loyalty toward Erica than I seemed to. I like Erica a lot. And I was certainly loyal to her when I was with her. And I was thinking about her when I was with Cindy and this afternoon in the booth at the SUNDAE SHOPPE with Kay and Cindy and Jennie. I didn't think about other girls when I was with her. Maybe that's all you can expect of a seventeen-year-old guy.

When I wasn't with Erica, I didn't have any trouble thinking about other girls. Here I was enjoying Cindy's company. And I knew that I would go on a date with Kay, the gorgeous redhead from this afternoon, in a second if I were given the opportunity. I even felt a brief moment of envy when Leon walked over with Lois. Why is it that when you're seventeen and you're with a pretty girl, you feel like you could spend the rest of your life with her, but when the next pretty girl comes along, you feel the same way about her?

CHAPTER 32

The Learning Curve

Cindy jolted me from my thoughts with the question I had been dreading. "Joey, can we go back to the roller coaster now? Then we can do the parachute jump and the Ferris wheel one more time before we go."

"Sure, Cindy," I said gamely. I walked with no great urgency toward the Ferris wheel, which seemed to be the farthest away.

"No, Joey, the roller coaster first. It's closer. And hurry or the park may close before we finish with all three."

I knew that. With resignation, I followed her as she ran toward the roller coaster. "Coming, Cindy." But I hoped for an early closing.

On the roller coaster I learned something. While waiting our turn, I noticed that some of the people on the roller coaster were holding their arms up over their head and yelling as they dropped into oblivion. What struck me was that they were all smiling. They were actually enjoying the ride. I attributed this to either a genetic defect on their part or that they knew something that I didn't. I decided to imitate their actions.

We were strapped into the car. The car moved slowly up the track to the top of the first hill. Just as it went over the top and started to plummet downward, I raised my arms over my head, closed my eyes, and yelled for all I was worth. It worked. My stomach did not revolt and the sense of free-fall was at least bearable. I was a bit concerned about the yell, however. To a bystander, it might sound a little like fear enhanced by terror. The fact that it was fear didn't matter; I just didn't want it to sound like fear.

I decided that from then on, when I yelled I would yell something meaningful like "Geronimo" or "Remember the Alamo" or "Bluegrass needs a banjo." By the final death-drop of the ride, I was able to fake a smile while I yelled. I was pleased with my discovery as well as with my clever modifications.

I could hardly wait for the parachute ride. "Come on, Cindy," I said eagerly. "Let's hurry. Maybe we can get back to the Scrambler before the park closes." I may have been pushing things a bit, but why not end the evening in the park with a ride where Cindy would be squeezed up close to me?

We quickly arrived at the parachute ride and Kong was still there. I decided to have some fun with him. After we were strapped in, and as we were being drawn slowly upward, I looked down at him and said, "Hey, mister. I just ate four hot dogs, some french fries, and a double chocolate shake and I don't feel too good. You better stand back." I could hear Cindy giggle as Kong looked up at me and the cigar fell out of his mouth. I thought I heard a little sailor language as he bent down, picked up the badly gnawed cigar, and reinserted it into his mouth. When I saw that, I thought I might actually throw up, but when Cindy said "Oh yuck!" all I could do was laugh.

We reached the top and were released for the drop. This time I knew what to expect. I reached up and grabbed the cords attached to the harness above me and yelled "Tierra del Fuego" because that was the first thing that came into my mind. I was really hitting my stride now. If we moved quickly, we could make it to the Ferris wheel and the Scrambler before the park closed. I didn't wait for Kong to unhitch me this time. He, however, was not satisfied to leave well-enough alone. "What's the hurry, kid?" he said, chewing with a vengeance on his cigar. "Did you lose it at the other end?" He gave a sinister laugh.

"No, mister," I said. "I'm fine. Say why don't you get a new cigar?"

"Why should I?" he answered. "This one's barely a week old."

Now I had a second good reason to move quickly to the Ferris wheel. I wondered how many citations a health inspector could write on that guy.

This time, the Ferris wheel ride was more pleasant for Cindy. As soon as we got in, I put my arm around her shoulder and she curled up against me with her head on my chest and her hand on my shoulder. She closed her eyes and seemed to be calm and relaxed. Her hair still smelled terrific. The breeze had a mildly cooling effect and the ride seemed to last only a few seconds. Actually, it had gone on for several minutes more than usual because it was the last ride of the night. It was announced that the park was closing for the night and of course we were invited back tomorrow night. We would miss a second ride on the Scrambler, but I had no complaints.

We sat in the chair waiting for the attendant to unlatch the bar. "Can we stay here like this for a while?" said Cindy dreamily. "I don't feel like moving."

"I wish we could," I said honestly, "but I'm afraid they'll bring Kong over here to kick us out if we don't move."

"Oh yuck!" she said disgustedly as she sat up quickly and exited the chair. "I think I'd rather babysit Frieda."

"That's a close call, but I think I'd probably pick Frieda too," I agreed. She laughed and we walked off toward the parking area. As we were nearing the gate, we saw Leon with Lois. They were tucked in behind one of the ticket booths and he was holding her in his arms like he meant business. She seemed to be in agreement since she had her arms locked around the back of his neck. Soon they released each other reluctantly, kissed briefly, and Lois ran off to meet her father and sister. Leon walked distractedly toward the gate but was still some distance away from us. "Well," I said to Cindy, "it looks like Leon has created quite a dilemma for himself. Will it be Lois or will it be Phyllis?"

"Yeah," responded Cindy. "Tune in next month and count the worry lines and the bruises." Then she added thoughtfully, "Maybe we better keep this to ourselves. He's got enough to worry about without having to try to explain it to us."

We met Leon back at the car. He hadn't noticed that we were just a little way behind him and he certainly didn't know that we had seen his farewell to Lois. "Hi, Leon," I said as we approached him at the car. "We had a great time. How about you?"

"Oh, it was pretty good," he said trying to sound nonchalant. "It was no big deal, though." He reached into the glove box and retrieved a small notebook and a pen. He wrote down what looked to be a phone number. He tore the slip of paper from the notebook and quickly slid it into his wallet. "Well, guys," he asked, "where do you want to go to eat? I vote for Big Patty's."

"Fine with me," I said agreeably. "How about you, Cindy?"

"It's unanimous. Let's go. I'm starved," she said.

Big Patty's was not as busy as it had been on our previous visit. We were able to park much closer to the entrance and there was no sign of the leather jackets, Pedro and Linus. However, Sue, alias Patty, was still waiting table when we entered. I took a quick look around to see if Fawn and Melissa were there. They weren't. I reminded Leon that we might have to go into our Brother Jonathan and Brother Simon routine if they showed up. Cindy wanted to know more about that. She laughed until tears streamed down her cheeks when I explained what had happened. We decided that if the girls showed up, we could still introduce Cindy as Brother Simon's (Leon's) sister. At least that would be the truth. Of course they probably wouldn't believe it.

After discussing possibilities for a few minutes, we figured that the worst they could do was try to report us to the rector of the seminary, which we did not attend in the first place. We considered trying to convince them that Cindy was studying to be a nun but decided against it because Cindy was wearing shorts and looked like she was having fun.

Patty, or Sue, came over to take our order. "Well, if it isn't Brother Simon and Brother Jonathan. Let me guess." She said pointing to Cindy, "This must be Sister Debbie." We must have all turned a deep red. She laughed and added, "Don't worry, kids. Your secret is safe with me. Besides, the two ladies in question have already been in and left. Same with Pedro and Linus. You're safe. Now, what'll you have?"

We all breathed a sigh of relief. With our safety thus guaranteed, our appetites grew. We ordered for five, Cindy choosing not to be a glutton. We filled in the time waiting for our food to arrive by telling stories about people we knew from school and the entertaining things they had done. Some of the stories may even have been true. I know at least one of mine was. But we had fun. We ate our fill and then talked some more. Even Leon seemed to enjoy Cindy's company. Of course I enjoyed it, but then, she wasn't my sister.

We drove home, still talking and laughing and at peace with the world. It was neat because nobody yelled at us, even though it was a little after midnight when we got home. I would have to remember to tell my mother about that when I got home. Yeah, right!

As I drifted off to sleep that night, my thoughts reviewed the events of the last several days. I thought of Mad Dog and the other guys I'd met, of ELF, the basketball game, the White Sox game, the fight, the softball game…And then my thoughts turned to Cindy, to Kay, and finally to Erica. My thoughts of Erica dissolved only as sleep took over.

CHAPTER 33

Shopping with Kay

After breakfast on Thursday morning, it occurred to me that Mom had told me to be sure to buy small thank-you gifts for Aunt Leona and Uncle Fred for inviting me to stay for a week. She also told me that it would be thoughtful to get something for each of the kids too. The thought of buying a gift for Frieda caused a feeling not unlike that of the flu.

Sister Evelyn had assured us in religion class last spring that if we accepted pain in our life without complaint and returned good to those who caused us pain, we guaranteed ourselves a place in heaven. I wasn't totally convinced that it was that simple, but I figured I had nothing to lose. Besides, there are certain things that it just doesn't make sense to disbelieve.

I decided that I needed help finding appropriate gifts. Since Erica was baby-sitting again and I certainly couldn't ask Cindy to help pick out her own gift, I decided to call Kay and ask her if she would be interested in helping me shop. I dialed Kay's number not knowing for sure what I would say. The phone was answered after two rings. "Hello, O'Toole's residence. Kay speaking."

"Hi, Kay," I said, trying to sound calm and confident. "This is Joey Winters. Remember? From the softball game yesterday."

"Of course I remember, Joey Winters." Even her voice on the phone sounded inviting. "I'm glad you called. What's up?"

"Well, Kay, I've got a small problem and I thought you might be able to help me out," I said.

"You're in luck. Thursday mornings just happen to be set aside to help out guys named Joey Winters," she said in a mock serious tone. Then she added in a much friendlier manner, "I'd love to help you, Joey, especially if it means that I get to see you again."

"Well, it does mean that," I said. "You see, I need to do some shopping for gifts for Aunt Leona, Uncle Fred, Leon, Cindy, and Frieda. I sure could use your help. I have no idea what they might like, except maybe for Leon, and I don't have the faintest notion where to shop."

"I have surely died and gone to heaven," she exclaimed. "I get to see you *and* go shopping. This is wonderful." She paused a moment, then said, "I know, let's go down to the Loop. There are hundreds of little shops as well as the big department stores. I know we can find something within your budget. We can take the bus downtown and back."

She gave me directions to her house, which was only a few blocks away, and we hung up. Leon had decided that the folk group needed more rehearsal and was making plans to go to Frank's house for the morning. He asked if I wanted to come along, but I told him that I had called Kay and was going over to see her. I told him we might go shopping so I'd see him later. Leon looked at me as though I had just given a hot-foot to the pope. "You mean that you're two-timing Erica?"

"Take it easy, Leon," I said. "I mean, I'm not going steady with her. Besides, Kay is going to help me buy a gift for Erica. I'm not very good at finding gifts." Actually I had no intention of asking Kay to help me find a gift for Erica, but it wouldn't be a bad idea for me to get something for Erica anyway.

"Oh, don't get me wrong." said Leon. "If I didn't already have Phyllis and I had to choose between Kay and Erica, it would be a tough choice. What the heck, you're only here for a week. It probably is kind of silly to expect that you'd get tied down to one girl in a week." He thought for a moment, then said, "You must be amazing back in

Benton Harbor. I'll bet you have *two* little black books. You are my hero. I mean that." All this coming from the guy who now had Lois on his dance card along with Phyllis.

"Well, my dating life isn't exactly inactive," I replied. The truth was that my dating life was practically non-existent. I'd had more dates this week than I'd had in the past three months back home. "I guess I do pretty well, but I don't have two little black books. Of course, I do write small in the one I have." Leon looked impressed with my false display of modesty. Sometimes a little creative fabrication can be fun.

Leon left for his final rehearsal and I walked the few blocks to Kay's house. I was feeling a little nervous when I got there. I guess I was concerned about what it would look like to Erica if word got back to her. Of course I had considered her first, but she was babysitting. I decided that I would tell her everything when I saw her tonight. I really did like her and I owed it to her to be honest. I still felt a little uncomfortable as I ascended the steps and rang the doorbell.

Every time I use a doorbell, I wonder if it works. It seems like half the time they don't work. I remember the first time I went out collecting when I had a paper route. Almost everybody had a doorbell but less than half worked. After a while I got to know which ones worked and which ones didn't, but it left me with a fear of doorbells whenever I go to an unfamiliar house. Fortunately this time I didn't have to decide whether to try again or knock. Kay opened the door about ten seconds after I rang the bell. Either it worked or she was watching out the window for me.

Kay looked beautiful. Her smile was bright and honest, her green eyes twinkled, and her long auburn hair had a graceful wave with loose curls at the end. I hadn't noticed how pretty her hair looked at the game because it was tied back and put up under her baseball cap. In addition to what I've already described, if you bothered to look below her neck, you would not be disappointed. And according to Cindy, she had a 3.9 grade point. Also, she seemed to like me, which made her very discerning in my book.

"Hi, Joey," she said cheerfully. "If we hurry, we can catch the next bus for the Loop. The bus stop is just down at the corner." She pointed out the direction and then called back into the house, "Bye, Mom. I'll be back by one o'clock." She closed the door, gave me a quick hug, and took my arm as we walked briskly to the corner.

When we reached the bus stop, we could see the bus about a block away. There would be no long wait this time. Kay had some tokens, which we deposited in the coin muncher as we boarded the bus. I had always been fascinated by the device that buses used for collecting money and tokens. I never fully understood what it did except that it seemed to make it easy for the driver to see if you had deposited the correct amount. Eventually he would flip a lever and all the money would drop out of sight.

We found two seats toward the middle of the bus, which was nearly full. It looked mostly like people who were going shopping or who could go to work whenever they felt like it. This bus was like all others I had experienced. Since we were facing the side of the bus, every time the bus started up we were pressed toward the back of the bus and every time it stopped we were thrown toward the front. As a result, almost from the beginning we were pushed together, and I guess we both decided, independently, that together was okay.

Kay seemed to enjoy the experience and had seated herself as close to me as possible to get the maximum benefit from the jostling. My arm seemed to be in the way. Not wishing to appear uncooperative, I moved my arm up over the back of the seat and let my hand fall lazily on her shoulder. She squeezed even closer. I guess that'll show me. I would have to remember to get a seat facing the side of the bus on the way home. This trip was becoming a real education. I'd never considered the advantages of seats facing the sides of the bus versus the seats facing the front of the bus before.

When we arrived in the Loop, I looked around to see that I was surrounded by huge buildings. Now, big in Benton Harbor was maybe six stories. In Chicago, the public restrooms were six stories. "Look over there, Joey," said Kay excitedly. "That's the Prudential Building. It's so tall that they say you can see the lights across the lake in Benton Harbor on a clear night. Maybe, if we have time after shopping, we can go up there and look."

"We'll have to make time," I said. "I've never been in a really tall building before. You know, I think you could put all the buildings in downtown Benton Harbor inside that building and still have room for the Democratic Convention."

"Then let's get shopping, Joey," said Kay enthusiastically. "You said you knew what you wanted to get for Leon. Why don't you tell me what it is and maybe we can start with that. I've got some ideas for the others too."

"Well, I thought I'd get Leon a record. He likes folk music and there must be a lot of things he doesn't have. I've already looked through his record collection."

"Good. There's a big record shop just around the corner. Let's start there. Besides, there are a couple of other stores in the same block where we can get the other gifts." Kay led me to the record store and we started browsing. I finally settled on a record by Oscar Brand. He was a handsome folk singer who was born in Canada and apparently was doing concerts and working in the United States. We took the record into a booth and listened to parts of several selections. There were tender ballads and several humorous tunes. He had a pleasant sound and I figured Leon would like the record. I was pretty sure he didn't have anything by Oscar Brand in his collection.

One purchase down and four (or five) to go. We went into several gift shops and seemed to be browsing although Kay probably knew what she was doing. In one shop we found a decorative, nylon scarf for Aunt Leona. Kay assured me that Aunt Leona would be thrilled with the scarf. Apparently they were the current high fashion-thing of the week. In another shop we found a daisy flower pin for Cindy. Apparently Kay had heard Cindy talk about hoping she would get one for her birthday in December. At the same shop we picked up some bubble bath powder for Frieda. I was secretly trying to figure out how to lace the bubble bath with itching powder.

Each gift was properly packaged and wrapped after each purchase. This was fortunate since anything that I wrapped looked like the winning result of a contest to see who could use the most Scotch tape. At least the light glistened off of any package I wrapped. It was also a good thing I had Kay with me. I never would have thought to ask to have the packages wrapped as gifts.

We still had to find a gift for Uncle Fred. First we looked in the Leather Shop that seemed to specialize in branding your monogram on wallets. The smell of burning leather filled the air. We decided against a purchase from this shop. Next we found a small costume jewelry shop that had some very nice pins, tie clasps, cuff links, and so on. We found a tie clasp and a pair of cuff links that we had monogrammed and wrapped for Uncle Fred. While the engraving was being done, Kay said, "I'm just going to look around to get some ideas for some future gifts. This would be a nice place for you to find a gift for Erica. Promise to let me see what you get." I stood there dumbfounded as she smiled, turned, and began looking around the store. I guess there were no secrets from that crowd. I spotted a nice gold-plated fine chain necklace and several types of pendants that could be added. I knew that Erica's birthday was in May, same as mine, so I found an emerald green stone (not a real emerald) and took it over to Kay. She nodded approvingly. "Nice choice. It's personal but not too personal. I know she will like it." Still reeling from the events of the last five minutes, I went back to the counter and had the clerk wrap the necklace as well.

I had accomplished my goal and still had some money left over. In one manageable bag I now carried all the gifts I needed. It was not quite lunchtime so we had plenty of time yet. I met back up with Kay and I had to ask, "How did you know?"

"I'm a girl. It's my job to know," she said cryptically. I made a mental note to always assume girls knew.

I offered to buy lunch so Kay guided me to a deli that specialized in kosher sandwiches. Kay said that this place was her favorite. She ordered corned beef on rye and I ordered turkey on whole wheat. The sandwiches came on a plate with potato chips and two large wedges of dill pickle. We each had a coke.

We found a small round table with two chairs across from each other. We enjoyed our meal and talked about school, summer, college plans, and just about anything else that popped into our heads. I kept trying to figure out a way to stay in Chicago for the summer. In less than a week I had at least met three absolutely gorgeous girls who didn't think I was a dipstick. Even if one of them was my cousin (but not blood-related), this was luck without match. None of the guys at school had even dreamed of this kind of luck. I'd better get pictures of each of these girls or nobody back home will believe me.

After we finished eating we went outside and looked around. Kay pointed to a very tall building and said, "Oh look, let's go there. We have enough time to see it before we catch the bus."

We went to the Prudential Building[3] and rode the elevator up to the observation deck at the top. The view was spectacular. You could see for miles in every direction. "Omigosh! Joey, look!" said Kay excitedly.

"What is it?" I asked.

She pointed down toward the street. "Look how high we are," she exclaimed. "It looks like a bunch of ants scurrying around down there."

She was right. I hadn't looked straight down until then. I wished I hadn't. I began to feel a little dizzy. I then began to worry that the glass would break and I would be sucked out, or that the wall would open up and I would fall. I stopped leaning against anything. Just then I heard a little kid ask the attendant about the wind. "Mister, it is true that the wind makes the building sway back and forth?" the kid asked.

"Yes, young man, it is," responded the attendant. "In fact, this building will sway almost a foot in either direction when the wind is strong. Today, however, you can't notice a thing. The wind isn't very strong and we are swaying only an inch or so." I knew he was lying. I could feel it swaying and it had to be at least an inch-and-a-half. Now I was beginning to feel sick.

"Look over there, Joey," said Kay. "I can see where we live. I mean, I can't see the actual house, but I can see the neighborhood. This is fun, isn't it, Joey?"

"I'll say. I've never experienced anything like this before," I said. It was time to be brave again. If I stood behind Kay and thought about how attractive she was, I could forget that we were about a million feet in the air with nothing but some puny steel and concrete to hold us up. That seemed to work.

Mercifully, Kay decided she had seen enough and that it was time to start back home. As we left the observation deck, I saw the little kid holding onto the railing and rocking back and forth. "Look, Mom," he said, "I'm making the building sway." I couldn't take much more. I sincerely hoped that my lunch and I would remain on good terms and return to the ground together.

---

[3] The Prudential Building was the tallest in Chicago in 1960. Eventually it would be surpassed by several other buildings including the Hancock Building and the Sears Towers.

We got on the elevator. I was not prepared for what followed. First of all, as the doors closed, I was convinced that the wind had picked up and the building was at maximum sway.

All of a sudden, the bottom seemed to come out of the elevator. We plummeted downward. My mind raced to remember how elevators had safety devices that made it impossible for them to break loose and go crashing to the ground. Whatever these devices were, this elevator didn't have them. We were all doomed. I began to wonder how far they would have to dig to find us after we hit bottom. All of a sudden the elevator began to slow down. We eased to a stop, the doors opened and I noticed the sign above the door, which said EXPRESS ELEVATOR. I had a sudden urge to tie myself to the nearest rock and stay there until I died, but I kept a smile on my face. "Gosh, that was fun, wasn't it, Kay?" I said as though I believed it.

"It was exhilarating, Joey," she said with glee. "Do you want to ride up and back down again?"

"It sounds tempting, Kay. Maybe if you'll promise to hold onto me tight on the way down as though you are scared. But really, I should be getting home."

"Oh, you're right," she said as she looked at the clock. "It's later than I thought. I have to get home and get some laundry done and then get ready for tonight. A bunch of us girls are going to a movie."

We found the correct bus stop and again had to wait less than two minutes for our bus. God must have figured I had done my penance at the Prudential Building because there were two seats empty facing the side of the bus. We assumed the sitting positions we had discovered this morning and enjoyed the ride back home. This time Kay rested her head on my shoulder. I couldn't think of any reason to object, so I didn't.

We arrived at our stop much too quickly. I considered writing to the Chicago Transit Authority to tell them that their driver drives too fast or doesn't make enough stops or something, but decided that it would be a waste of time. I walked Kay to her house. When we arrived, she hung onto my arm and pulled me into the house. "My mom's still home, Joey," she said. "I see her car is still in the garage. I want her to meet you. Besides I have to run upstairs to get that picture you asked for."

I followed her in and met her mother. She seemed very pleasant and friendly. She was also very attractive for being a teenager's mother. She asked me about school and shopping and all kinds of other things while Kay was gone to get the picture. I must admit, though, that she made me feel relaxed and it was fun talking to her.

Soon Kay came back downstairs with a picture that did her justice and would make me the envy of all of my male classmates. We talked with her mother a few more minutes and then Kay walked me to the front door. In the foyer, Kay gave me a big hug and a kiss. "I really enjoyed today, Joey. Thanks for calling. And the next time you're in Chicago, give me a call." she said.

"Thanks, Kay," I replied. "I really enjoyed being with you too. I certainly have good reason to come back. Everyone has been so nice and friendly." I gave her another quick hug. "Thanks for all your help," I said, looking at the bag I carried. "I don't know what I would have done without you."

"See you, Joey," she called out the door as I walked down the steps toward the sidewalk. I turned and waved. "Enjoy the pool party tonight," she added before closing the door.

Again I was nonplussed. She did know everything. I was beginning to realize that not only was I confused, I probably would be for the rest of my life.

I was a little sad that this part of the day was ending but I was looking forward with excitement to the pool party (that everyone seemed to know about) tonight. In my thoughts Erica still took first place.

CHAPTER 34

The Pool Party

The afternoon was relatively quiet. I shot baskets in the driveway with Leon and Cindy. I played Parcheesi with Cindy while Leon ironed for the third time the shirt he was going to wear for ELF's professional debut. The three of us sat around talking about the past week and reliving some of the more exciting events. In all we had a great time. Before supper, I called Erica to ask her to bring a picture of herself that I could take home with me. She agreed and asked if I had one to give her. I told her that I just had a school picture with me but she could have it. I promised to send her a better one when I got back to Benton Harbor. We were anxious to see each other.

After I had eaten an early supper I showered, shaved, combed, sprayed, powdered, brushed, dressed, and redressed. Finally, at 5:59 p.m., I was ready for what promised to be the best date of my life. Now I had approximately eleven minutes to wait for Erica if she was on time. I tried to maintain a calm exterior even though I was a nervous wreck. Everything I wore seemed to be too tight or too loose.

I stepped back into the bedroom to take another look in the full-length mirror. Everything seemed to be okay. Colors didn't clash. My arms had gone through the correct sleeves, there was one leg in each pant leg, and the zipper of my jeans was in front and zipped. So far, so good. However, as I continued to look in the mirror, my shoes just didn't look right. They matched. That was a start. I looked directly at the shoes. Good grief, I had them on the wrong feet. I couldn't believe it. I sat on the edge of the bed and changed them. It was a good thing I hadn't gone downstairs like that. Frieda would probably have noticed and split a gut laughing.

Finally I was ready. It's amazing how everything feels wrong when your shoes are on the wrong feet. Once I had corrected the problem, everything felt much better. I tried to give the appearance of confidence as I walked downstairs. It was a mistake. My heel caught on the next to last step and my knees started to buckle. From this point on, a calm appearance was impossible. I was fighting to avoid falling flat on my face. As a result of over-correcting, I fell instead on my behind. Of course Frieda was right there and presented me with hysteria in pantomime. She must have known that if Uncle Fred or Aunt Leona caught her making fun of me, she would be grounded for longer than eternity. I could just picture St. Peter saying to her, "Sorry, Frieda. I can't let you in. You're still grounded." She would be doomed to the waiting room for all eternity.

I was embarrassed but at least her glee had to be contained. As I got back to my feet, Cindy came past the stairs on her way to the family room to watch TV. She stopped a moment and looked at me. She obviously hadn't seen my display of grace and coordination. "Gee, Joey, you look really handsome." She stepped a little closer and sniffed. "And you smell nice too. What is that aftershave you're wearing?"

"It's just Old Spice," I said. "Do you really like it?" If she liked it, maybe Erica would like it.

"Oh yes!" she replied warmly. "It really smells nice." The unsolicited testimonial built my confidence.

"Thanks, Cindy," I said. "By the way, could I get a picture of you tomorrow before I leave? I keep forgetting to ask. I want to show all the guys back home what a pretty cousin I have."

"Sure, Joey," She was blushing. "Gee, thanks for the compliment." Frieda was now gagging in pantomime.

"It wasn't a compliment, Cindy. It was the truth," I said as I leaned over and gave her a kiss on the cheek. Now Frieda was mimicking severe stomach cramps. I was beginning to feel that pantomime should be encouraged among younger children. It was easier not to look than it was not to listen. It also seemed to take more effort, which would cause them to tire sooner.

I was about to follow Cindy into the family room when I heard a car pull into the driveway. It had to be Erica. "Bye everyone," I called. "Erica is here."

I was out the door and halfway down the steps when Uncle Fred opened the door and said, "Wait a minute, Joey. Just in case you are late getting back, here's a key." He was detaching a key from his key ring. As he handed me the key he said, "Have a good time, Joey." I was absolutely amazed. This exchange could never have occurred between my parents and me at home. I'll bet it never occurred between Uncle Fred and Leon either. I hoped that Leon had not been watching.

"Thanks, Uncle Fred," I said as I walked toward the car in the driveway. Erica had just gotten out and was walking toward me. At first I couldn't figure out why. "Hi, Joey," she said cheerfully as she approached. She looked even better than I remembered. She was wearing a pair of pink shorts, a white, loose-fitting blouse, and sandals. Her hair was pulled back in a pony-tail that had a large, soft, spiral curl and had a fascinating bounce to it with each step she took. Her smile was bright, her eyes sparkled, and I was mesmerized.

She walked right up to me, gave me a hug, kissed me on the cheek, and handed me the car keys. I tried to regain a calm exterior. (Inside it was hopeless.) "Hi, Erica," I said as I took the keys. "Gosh, you look great tonight." Realizing that it could be taken the wrong way, I added, "Again!"

"Thanks, Joey." Her face reddened slightly. She put her arm around mine and we walked toward the car. I opened the passenger door and I could smell her perfume as she stepped in front of me to get in. I walked around to the driver's side and tossed my towel in the backseat beside hers. She was already in the middle of the front bench seat as I got in and put the key in the ignition. I looked quickly at the column. It was an automatic. I was glad. I didn't really want to try to impress her with my ability to drive a stick.

The car started on the first try. I pulled out of the drive and followed her directions to the house where the party would be. She left a couple of inches between us, enough room that I could easily use both hands on the steering wheel. The car did not have power steering. I decided that I had better keep both hands on the wheel and I interpreted the small gap she left between us as an unspoken suggestion.

As we pulled alongside the curb near the house, Erica slid a little closer. I removed the key from the ignition, put my arm around her, and rested my hand on her right shoulder. She placed her head on my shoulder and put her right hand on my chest. After a few moments she looked up at me and said, "With a little luck, Joey, maybe this night will never end."

"I could handle that," I said, knowing that this was a statement of absolute truth. I remembered a class in school last spring when the young assistant pastor had talked to us about Aristotle, Plato, and something called absolute truth. I figured we weren't expected to understand it at the time. Now I did.

I looked into her eyes. After a few moments I decided not to find out who would blink first. Instead, I closed my eyes and kissed her. She kissed back. (I assumed her eyes were closed too. I was tempted to open mine and see. I began to wonder if she could tell that I was opening my eyes. What if she opened hers after I opened mine and saw that mine were opened? What would she say? What would she think? What a stupid thing to be thinking about when you're kissing someone as special as Erica.) The thought disappeared but the kiss lingered. Finally the need to breathe gained the upper hand and we separated. "We'd better get in to the party although I think I'd rather stay right here," said Erica softly.

"Okay, let's go in," I said. "I want to make all the other guys jealous." One more quick kiss and I opened the door and grabbed the towels. I went around the back of the car and opened her door, she got out and we walked to the front door. Amy, who was hosting the party, met us at the door. She was a cute blond wearing a neon green two-piece bathing suit and a guy named Mike on her arm. I'm not sure which clung more tightly. "Hi Erica!" she bubbled. "So this is Joey. He's cute. Hi, Joey. This is Mike. Come on through the house to the pool. If you need to change, the boys are changing down the hall and the girls are changing upstairs." She stopped and took a breath. I was relieved. I breathed too. She continued, "Mom said we had to use two separate rooms for changing." She giggled as she bounced through the house. Mike grinned but kept pace, never letting loose of her arm. Amy's parents were in the living room watching TV so we stopped and said hello to them. Since Erica and I had both worn our swim suits to the party, we followed Amy and Mike out to the pool. The pool area was beautiful. The oval-shaped pool was surrounded by a brick courtyard, which was enclosed by a redwood privacy fence. There were five other couples that I hadn't met yet, and at the moment they were all in lounging chairs or seated around a picnic table playing euchre. Amy (with Mike still attached) took us around and introduced me to everyone. I tried to remember who everyone was by memorizing pairs of names and the color of the girl's bathing suit. Fortunately they were all different. (Both the colors and the names.) There were Stan and Charlotte (gold and black one-piece), Tom and Edna (pink and gray one-piece), Gordon and Angie (white with green polka dots two-piece), Bob and Mindy (bright yellow bikini), and finally, Phil and Sarah (azure blue one-piece). Erica quietly promised to help me keep track since she already knew everybody from school except for Gordon.

Sarah and Phil invited us to come and sit with them. Amy handed us each a bag into which we could put our clothes. She had arranged it so there was a different color pair of bags for each couple. Ours was purple. Amy and Mike ran off to the kitchen to arrange snacks or whatever. I was beginning to wonder if Amy and Mike were Siamese twins. We found a table where people seemed to have deposited towels and the colorful clothing bags. Erica and I set down our towels and removed our outer clothing, putting it into our purple bags. When I was finished, I looked back at Erica. She was standing there putting her feet back into her sandals. She had on a very flattering one-piece suit. It was kelly green with a wide silver band that went diagonally from her left breast to the top of her right thigh. She was gorgeous. I said the only thing that came to mind. "WOW!" I meant it.

"That was the idea, Joey," she said with a triumphant smile on her face. "You are supposed to keep your eyes on me tonight and not all those other beautiful girls."

"Erica," I said in awe, "it's no contest. My problem is that the other guys are going to be looking at you too."

"Maybe you could growl at them," she suggested. *Maybe I could*, I thought.

We rejoined Sarah and Phil and talked about a variety of things. It turned out that Phil and I had at least one thing in common: we both wanted to attend the University of Notre Dame. Sarah wanted to go to Xavier College on the south side of Chicago. We continued a lengthy discussion of the problems of selecting and applying to various colleges. After a couple of minutes, I noticed that Erica was staying kind of quiet on the subject. Apparently Sarah noticed as well. "Have you decided on any schools yet, Erica?" she asked.

"No," she said unenthusiastically. "I really haven't been able to make up my mind. I suppose I should work a little harder on it."

I got the impression that I should change the subject. "How come nobody's swimming yet? Is the water too wet?" I asked.

It grew deathly silent. Everybody was looking at me with grins growing into full-blown smiles. All the guys (except Mike who seemed permanently grafted to Amy) got up and walked over toward me. I didn't like the looks of it. I started to get up but Phil was standing behind me and he put his hands on my shoulders. "Relax, Joey," he said.

The other guys all arrived together. "Here he is guys." shouted Gordon. "Into the drink with him." At that they picked me up and carried me to the deep end of the pool. I was given the old heave-ho. In mid-air I tried to straighten out, clasp my hands behind my head, and look like I was relaxing in a hammock. When I hit the water, I was surprised to find that it was not very cold. In fact, it was quite comfortable. By now everyone was at poolside. I swam back to the edge of the pool and reached up to Erica, seeking help getting out of the pool. She took my hand and I pulled back. In she went. As soon as she hit the water, everyone else jumped in. She surfaced beside me, laughing. "I guess I should have told you," she admitted. "Whenever there is a pool party, we all stay out of the pool until somebody mentions something about swimming or water or the pool. Then we throw that person in. I think we all knew it would probably be you or Gordon and it looks like Angie warned Gordon. I guess you were doomed. Sorry."

"Interesting custom," I acknowledged. "But what happens if nobody says anything?"

"Oh, we have that covered," she said. "If nobody is in the pool by seven thirty, the host or hostess rings a bell and everybody is supposed to jump in."

By now it was a free-for-all. People were jumping in, getting pushed in, dragging themselves out, and jumping back in. Even Amy and Mike were in the pool, though they still seemed to be attached. Tom and Stan got out and set up a net across the pool and we divided up into teams. Playing volleyball in the water is a little more difficult than playing on sand, especially if your side is at the deep end, but it was lots of fun. We traded sides after each game. After a little over an hour, my team was determined to be the champions of the solar system minus Pluto. About half of us didn't believe that Pluto was a planet anyway. We would play for the championship of the known universe after we regained our strength by demolishing the food supply.

While we had been playing, Amy's mom and dad had brought out the food. The picnic table was piled high with hot dogs, potato chips, baked beans, a tray of cut vegetables with a sour cream dill dip, bottles of pop, plates of cookies and a large sheet cake. "Come and get it," Amy's mom called as she stepped back, apparently in self-defense. And come and get it they did.

Even though I was dreaming of being a champion of the known universe in two sports, I stayed behind to offer my hand to Erica as she got out of the pool. Even with a wet pony-tail, she was gorgeous. When she was half-way up the ladder, she pulled me into the pool. "Now we're even, Joey," she said sweetly. By the time I got back out of the pool, I was at the very end of the food line. Mercifully Erica had waited for me and held out a paper plate for me. I had never seen food disappear so fast. After filling our plates I looked back at the table. It was nearly bare. Of course, we did have to rebuild our strength. Erica and I again sat with Sarah and Phil. This time we were also joined by the gold and black one-piece suit. That would be Charlotte and Stan. Talk tended to center around humorous events of the last school year. I probably enjoyed it more than the others because all of these were new stories to me. I did notice, however, that Mad Dog Norkus was mentioned in more than one story. I even told a couple of Lumpy Furgeson stories.

CHAPTER 35

The Bomb

By the time we finished eating, everybody had pretty well dried off. Nobody was particularly anxious to go back in the water. It was decided that we would move the tables and chairs to one side of the pool and bring out a record player so we could dance on the other side. First, though, we decided to change out of our semi-dry swimsuits into dry clothing. Erica asked me to walk her out to the car so she could get her hairbrush out of her purse. We picked up our towels and clothes bags, I fished the car keys from my jeans and we went out to the car holding hands. The sky was mostly clear with a few long thin wispy clouds near the horizon and sun was setting. The western horizon was a mixture of rich golds, vibrant oranges, and vivid reds. We stopped and stared as we reached the car. "Isn't the sky beautiful, Joey?" asked Erica softly.

"Yeah," I said, "but it begs to be shared. I'm glad you're here to share it with me." I stood behind her and put my arms around her waist. She put her hands on mine and leaned her head back against my chest. Her hair was still damp but I didn't mind. Her closeness was all that was important. That and the sunset that we claimed as ours.

"In a few minutes it'll be gone," she reflected with a hint of sadness in her voice.

"Yes," I said, "but it can remain in our memory if we want it to."

"Oh, Joey, why do the really beautiful things in life last such a short time?"

"I'm not sure, Erica. I sometimes think that God is teasing us with short glimpses of eternity. The beauty of this sunset will last forever even though the sunset itself will not. I think that beautiful things fade away to make room for greater beauty. You know, this sunset would not be as beautiful as it is to me if we were not here together to share it."

"I think I'm going to cry," she said. And she did. So did I, but I tried not to let her see.

Before long the colors bled together and then faded to a pale yellow. I opened the car door and Erica retrieved the brush from her purse. Then she pulled the pony-tail clip from her hair, shook her head to loosen the wet hair, and tossed the clip into her purse before shutting the car door. I couldn't put it off any longer.

"Erica, I need to tell you something," I said trying to remember what I had rehearsed a dozen times this afternoon. "You remember that there was a softball game yesterday."

"Of course, Joey. I was invited too but by the time I got home from shopping, it was too late. How was the game? I hope you enjoyed it."

"We had a great time. I guess you know everybody who was there."

"I'm sure I do. I'll bet you met Kay who is a shoo-in for class flirt at our school and will probably go to the national championships."

"As a matter of fact I did. And she certainly lived up to your assessment."

"Let me guess, she picked you as her target. I hope you didn't give her too hard a time. She's really a very nice person."

"Well, she did. That's what I wanted to talk to you about. This morning I needed to go get some gifts for Aunt Leona, Uncle Fred, Leon, Cindy, and Frieda as a thank-you for having me stay the week. I had no idea where to go or what to get, and I couldn't ask you because you were babysitting today. Obviously I couldn't ask Cindy since one gift would be for her. I ended up calling Kay to help me and she did. And she was really very helpful. She thought of details like having the store wrap the packages that never would have occurred to me."

"And you didn't think I would be angry or upset by this?" she asked.

"Whether you are or you aren't, I thought you had a right to know and that I should tell you. I hope you're not too upset. That would really bother me. Besides, I don't believe Kay had any designs on me. She seems to have too much fun flirting and playing the field."

"Joey, after you made this sunset so wonderful for me, how could I possibly be upset with you? Actually you have Kay pegged pretty well. She enjoys being with the person she is with but tomorrow it will be someone different. She is a lot of fun, though, isn't she?"

"I'm not sure I want to answer that. I will say that you are certainly a lot of fun, and the outstanding girl memories I take home from this trip will all be about you." Perhaps I might have a career in diplomacy.

We walked back through the house. At the foot of the stairs Erica gave me a light kiss. "Thank you for everything, Joey," she said quietly before going upstairs to change. I watched her until she was out of sight and then went to the room down the hall where the guys were changing. Most of them were finished and had left. Soon I was alone in the room. I checked the pocket of my jeans for the package that contained the necklace I had bought for Erica. It was still there. I decided to take it out to the car and hide below the driver's seat. While I was there, I deposited my towel on the backseat. I took one last look at what had been the sunset. It was gone. The beauty remained only in my memory. And in Erica's.

I returned to the pool. The music had started and several couples were dancing. Erica had not come downstairs yet. It was just as well. They weren't playing the music for slow dancing yet and I felt clumsy trying to dance fast. The people sat around drinking pop or juice and talking quietly. I sat down at a table by myself and wondered if I could remember the other couples. Part of my memory device had been the color of the girl's swimsuit and everyone had changed out of their swimsuits. Somebody put on the first slow music of the night. It was Elvis Presley's "Love Me Tender." Everyone got up and danced. I looked toward the door just in time to see Erica pass through it. Her hair must be naturally curly because it looked as it had earlier. It still had that springy bounce to it although it was no longer in a pony-tail. She walked over to me, put her arms around my neck as I put my arms around her waist, and we began to dance. It was slow music from then on. We danced for at least an hour non-stop. While I held Erica close, I could not get the image of the sunset out of my mind. Not that I wanted to.

Finally we sat down to take a breather. About half the couples were dancing and the rest were sitting around tables. The couples were sitting closer to each other and farther from the others than earlier in the evening. Erica and I talked about forgettable things. It was not so much that we wanted to remember what we said; rather, we wanted to hear and remember the gentleness of the other's voice.

It was a little past eleven when we left the party. We went to a city park near Uncle Fred's house. It was a place where young people tended to gather at night after a movie or pizza. It was a place where you could walk in the moonlight or sit on a park bench. We walked for a bit hand-in-hand. After about ten minutes we found an unoccupied bench near a large pond in the center of the park. We exchanged pictures as we had promised to do earlier. The moonlight was not sufficient to see the detail of her picture, but I could tell that it was her and that she looked beautiful. It captured her wonderful smile perfectly. I placed the picture carefully in my wallet and took out the small package that I retrieved from the under the driver's seat when we arrived at the park. "Erica." She looked at me with sadness in her eyes. "This isn't anything big or expensive. It just reminded me of you when I saw it this morning and I hope you will wear it occasionally and remember me." I handed her the package.

She carefully unwrapped it and held the necklace up to the moonlight. "Oh, Joey!" she exclaimed. "It's beautiful!" She turned her back to me and handed me the necklace. "Here, help me put it on." She held her hair up away from her neck while I fastened the clasp. Then she turned back toward me and melted into my arms. "But even without the necklace, I could never forget you." We kissed. Suddenly she pressed her face against my chest and began to cry. "Oh, Joey. I'm never going to see you again."

"Come on now, Erica," I said gently. "Benton Harbor isn't all that far away. We could see each other at holiday times or during summer vacations. In fact, I was hoping that you could come over and go to our homecoming dance in October. Do you think your parents would let you?"

"Oh, Joey!" she said, still crying. "You don't understand. I'm not going to be in Chicago. About ten weeks ago I found out that my dad was transferred to Seattle. We leave in August. That's why I'll never see you again."

I was in shock. I had expected a separation, but not this. "There's got to be a way for us to get together, Erica." I knew I was grasping for any hope. "Maybe I can go to college in Washington or maybe you can go to college here in the Midwest. Maybe when I'm in college, I can go out to Seattle and find a summer job."

"No, Joey!" she said firmly. "I want that as much as you do, but I know it won't happen. Joey, it's two thousand miles away. You'll go home tomorrow and soon you'll forget about me. Let's not raise false hopes." There were still tears on her cheeks.

"That doesn't have to happen, Erica," I pleaded. "We'll write letters. I'll call you every month."

"I know you will, Joey. And I'll write to you too. But after a while, the distance will overcome one or both of us. One of us would miss a letter and then two. And the other one of us would be hurt. It hurts now, Joey. Let's not drag it out. Let's admit that there is almost no chance that we will ever see each other again. If we admit that, to ourselves especially, then at least we won't feel too guilty when it happens. If we admit that, then I think I could bear waiting for your letters and phone calls knowing that someday they will probably stop. We'd still be friends, maybe more than friends, but there'd be no false commitments. It's like the sunset, Joey. It's here for a while and then it's gone. Its beauty is absolute and will always remain in your memory and in mine, but maybe that's enough. Like you said, it makes way for something even more beautiful."

"I don't want to admit that you're right," I said softly. "But I understand what you are saying. I want it to be wrong. I want us to be the exception. I can't give up."

"Oh Joey, you're a hopeless romantic. And that's what I love about you. I guess I'm too practical sometimes and I want to be a romantic too. You be the romantic for both of us, Joey. For me, it hurts too much now to let it keep on hurting. For me there can be peace only when I accept what is most likely going to happen. I'm sorry, Joey. It's what I must do."

"I won't argue with you, Erica. You're right. I am a romantic. And lots of times things don't work out that way. But I'll keep on trying because one time it will work. And that's the time that makes all the others worthwhile. There is one thing we can do. We can enjoy the sunset while it's there. We have now. The future is unreachable and the past is irretrievable but we have now." I reached out toward her and she came into my arms. Our lips met tenderly and then parted. She rested her head on my shoulder. I brushed my fingers through her silken hair. Each strand was more precious to me than gold. I hated time. My past did not know her, and my future robbed me of her. Only that small fragment of time called "now" had value.

After about twenty minutes, Erica looked up at me. "Tell me the truth. Did Kay pick out the necklace?" she asked with a quirky smile.

"I can honestly say that she did not. We were in the store getting a gift for Uncle Fred and I was trying to figure out how to get away from her so I could find something for you. In her defense, she did say out of the blue 'This would be a good place to find a gift for Erica. Promise to let me see what you get.' And then she went off to browse," I said.

"Good. I guess I'll let her live," said Erica and we both cracked up.

We got up and walked slowly back to the car, stopping frequently to embrace or kiss. Her tears had dried. Mine were yet to come.

CHAPTER 36

The Kings of Summer

It was a dismal Friday morning when I got out of bed. Between Leon's snoring and the bleak mood I was in when I got back to the house last night, I was unable to sleep. Leon was already up and had gone downstairs. I glanced out the window. The sky matched my mood. It was dark and gray with blackening clouds that threatened a downpour any moment. There was even lightning off in the distance.

I dressed quickly in the last clean pair of jeans and polo shirt I had, put on my sneakers, and began to pack my things for the journey home later this morning. I was going to wear socks, but I discovered that Freida the Freak had put Vaseline in the only clean socks I had left. I didn't care. I had already planned a final, all-out strike against her, which wouldn't even be noticed until well after I left.

As I packed I tried to get control of my mood. I didn't want to seem disappointed when I went downstairs. After all, everyone except Frieda had done everything possible to make my stay enjoyable. And, all in all, I'd had a wonderful time. What happened last night wasn't anybody's fault and it was best I kept it to myself.

I'd just finished packing when Cindy came by the room and looked in. "Joey," she said, "can I come in for a minute?"

"Oh sure, Cindy," I replied. "Come on in. I was just finishing my packing."

She walked over to me and put her arms around me and said, "I'm sorry, Joey. I know about Erica moving, but she didn't want me to say anything until after she told you. She said she would tell you last night after the party. She told me that moving to Seattle really hadn't bothered her too much until she met you. I know she likes you a lot. I wish it didn't have to happen." She just held onto me for a minute or so and I returned the light pressure. It was comforting to know that someone else knew about what had happened and cared. And that I didn't have to explain it.

"Thanks, Cindy. You know, you're a real neat cousin. I guess I need somebody to care. I'm glad it's you." I gave her an extra squeeze and stood back. Then I couldn't help it. I did explain it. I told Cindy all about last night: the good, the bad and the gruesome. I told her about the party, the sunset and our special claim to it, and finally about our differing viewpoints on the future. "In some ways I know Erica is right. I mean, we are only seventeen and there is still so much more to learn and experience in life. I'll admit that the odds don't favor a future for me with Erica in it. But I'm not ready to give up on that entirely. And if you say a word of this to any adult, I'll deny it. Besides, I am a romantic as charged. And for a romantic, there is hope—hope before the hurt, and hope after the hurt. After the hurt is gone, what remains is hope."

I reached down and picked up the greased socks, not sure I should pack them. "Look at this, Cindy. Satan's munchkin strikes again."

"You're kidding," she said with surprise. "Doesn't she ever learn? What is that?"

"I assume it's Vaseline," I replied. "I'm just trying to figure out a way to get them home without messing up everything in my bag. Got any ideas?"

"Yes, I do." There was a mischievous look in her eyes. "Leon has several pair of socks just like these. We'll just do a trade. Frieda has to do the laundry for the rest of the month anyway. She may get another month when Mom finds out she did this. And Leon will make sure that Mom finds out. This one will really backfire on her."

"Not only that," I added, "but I plan to strike one final blow before I go. I looked in her room yesterday and it's immaculate. What happened, a reverse earthquake?"

"Mom made her clean the room after the business with the catsup and mustard. Now she keeps it spotless. She makes her bed first thing in the morning and doesn't go in there the rest of the day until it's time to go to bed. I think she's afraid to let anything get out of order anymore."

"Good," I said. "I should be back in Benton Harbor by the time she finds out what I've done. I'm going to tell her I've set a trap for her and sooner or later she will spring it and then she's in for a terrible surprise. The truth is, I'm not going to do anything—no trap, nothing. It should keep her on her toes for a while. If she tries to tell anyone, it will just look like she's still trying to get me in trouble." We both chuckled about that as we left the room and went downstairs. I felt a little better and I had clean socks on my feet. I carried the small bag with the gifts I had purchased the day before. I figured I could pass them out at breakfast.

I was relieved to find that Aunt Leona had prepared breakfast. At least there would be no surprises this time. Everything looked good too. Though my spirits had a lid imposed by the news of last night, they were beginning to pick up. We all seated ourselves at the table and said grace. Then Uncle Fred started passing the egg platter and soon all plates were full and we were quietly eating. I remembered that ELF performed their first "concert" last night and asked, "Leon, how did your job go last night?"

"It went pretty well, Joey," he said with visible satisfaction. "The kids seemed to enjoy the singing and they really liked the jokes. The parents were so pleased that they gave us an extra five bucks. We had enough for an extra pizza and another pitcher of pop. We stayed at the pizza place for two hours. Now the guys want to line up some more jobs. I think we have to learn some more songs first. Anyway, we had a great time. How was the pool party, Joey?"

I noticed Cindy cringe as he asked. "Oh, it was great, Leon." I refused to let a great week end badly. "Erica and I had a really great time. I'm really going to miss her. You know, Leon, I don't think I've ever had so much fun and met so many really neat people as I have this week. I really want thank all of you for inviting me over. I got a little something for each of you yesterday because I really wanted to say thank you." I passed out the gifts and they each unwrapped theirs.

"Joey!" cried Aunt Leona, holding up the scarf. "It's beautiful. I have several outfits that this will go with. Thank you."

Leon was next. He held up the album. "This is great, Joey. I just heard about Oscar Brand last week. They played one of his songs on the radio and I really like his style. After breakfast, let's go upstairs and listen to it," I agreed. I wanted to hear the rest of it too.

Frieda opened hers and looked skeptical. "Well, it looks like bubble bath powder. What did you do, Joey, mix it with itching powder?"

"You figured me out, Frieda," I said. "That's just what I did. But don't worry, I don't think the itching powder can work on lizard skin." Even Uncle Fred smiled at that.

"Frieda!" scolded Aunt Leona. "Honestly, you say the most terrible things. I'm sorry, Joey. Sometimes I don't know what I'm going to do with her."

Uncle Fred was next. Showing her his tie clasp and cuff links he said, "Look, Leona. They're engraved with my initials too. Thank you, Joey."

Finally Cindy unwrapped her package. "Mom, look!" she shrieked with excitement. "Oh Joey, I've wanted a daisy pin for such a long time. Thank you!" She jumped up and gave me an enthusiastic hug.

"I have to admit that I had some help. Yesterday morning, when I was gone, Kay and I took the bus to the Loop and she helped me pick the gifts out. She was really a big help." I admitted.

"Did she help you pick out a gift for Erica too?" kidded Leon.

Remembering what I had told him I responded. "Actually she didn't. I did that on my own. But Kay did ask to see it after I picked it out. I had to tell you something yesterday, Leon. I didn't want you to know what I was really doing yet."

"I didn't know you went down to the Loop with Kay," said Cindy with surprise.

"That's probably the only thing you didn't know," I said, winking at her. She caught my meaning and winked back.

"Well, Joey, I don't care if you did have some help. In fact I'm impressed. Your gifts are so thoughtful and well chosen. You're a joy to have as a house guest."

"Well thank you, Aunt Leona. I really enjoyed staying with you. Maybe Leon and Cindy could come over at Christmas break. I'll ask Mom."

Leon and I went upstairs to listen to the record and to get my bags. Uncle Fred took the day off from work. He figured the rain would keep him from getting any outdoor work done and his office manager could take care of any calls. My train was to leave at eleven fifteen so we had an hour before we had to leave the house. During one of the songs I had heard the day before, I went down to see Frieda in the laundry room and give her the bad news about my trap. I got back up to Leon's room by the middle of the next song, which I had also heard. Then we listened to another record and talked about the past week until it was time to go.

Uncle Fred, Leon, and Cindy drove me to the train station and I got a big surprise as we drove through the neighborhood and passed Mad Dog's house. On the porch Mad Dog was playing checkers with Mr. Shaker and the bulldog was lying on Mad Dog's feet under the table asleep. They seemed to be having a great time. Every time I see Mad Dog I am more impressed.

We arrived in plenty of time and sat on a long bench in the station waiting for my departure to be called. "You know, Joey," said Cindy, "you and Leon better enjoy this summer vacation. This is the summer before your senior year. Next summer, all you'll have to look forward to is being a freshman again."

"You know, you're right," I said. "This summer it's like we are kings awaiting the glory of our senior year. Next summer, we'll just be peasants again. Then some kids a year younger than us will be kings." I looked at Cindy. "And queens," I added. It didn't seem fair. I didn't feel much like a king, but I'd have to get over that. I couldn't waste a whole great summer moping around about bad fortune. Still, I wouldn't give up on Erica. Somehow, I'd find a way.

The departure of my train was called and we walked toward the gate. Uncle Fred shook my hand and said, "Have a good trip, Joey. Maybe you can come again next summer. We enjoyed having you."

"Thanks, Uncle Fred," I said. "I really had a great time."

Leon took my hand next and shook it vigorously. "Farewell, King Joey," he said.

"And farewell to you, King Leon. I expect to see ELF on television before long."

Cindy gave me a hug and a kiss on the cheek. "Good bye, Joey. I really had fun at Riverview. Thanks." She paused and smiled. "And I'm sure Frieda will never forget you either." she said with a wink.

"Bye, Cindy," I said. "Now I know at least one cute cousin. I meant what I said about Christmas. I hope you and Leon can come."

I picked up my battered suitcase and boarded the train. It was just one short week ago that I had gotten off the train for my visit. I felt as though I was a very different person at the end of that week. There was a scar, but it was surrounded by blessings. And the blessings were many. I felt like I had found many new friends and I had discovered that people I didn't know liked me when they met me. I must be okay, especially if girls as cute, and more importantly, as nice as Erica, Kay and Cindy liked me. I had worried about that quite a bit. In another year I would be going off to college. Now I was confident that I could make new friends and meet girls. Who knows, I might even learn something in the classroom.

I found a seat and put my bag in the overhead compartment. I looked out the window and spotted my send-off party of three. They waved and I waved back. The train started to move. Leon and Uncle Fred and walked toward the parking lot. Cindy stayed and continued to wave until I could no longer see her. Soon the view through the window was obscured by a torrent of rain. Too tired to deal with the problems of the moment, I turned my thoughts to the possibilities of my reign as one of the kings of summer.

About The Author

(photo by Camille Coleman)

James Waner lives in Clio, Michigan with his wife Carol. They have three grown children and eight grandchildren. He is a retired Catholic school teacher of advanced chemistry, physical science and theology. You can write to him at jwaner5943@gmail.com